JESSIE
AND
THE RANGER

Other books by Cheri Jetton:

Blue Plate Special
Texas Dawn

JESSIE
AND
THE RANGER

•

Cheri Jetton

AVALON BOOKS
NEW YORK

PRINTED IN THE UNITED STATES OF AMERICA
ON ACID-FREE PAPER
BY HADDON CRAFTSMEN, BLOOMSBURG, PENNSYLVANIA

This one is for my son, John,
who works twelve-hour shifts keeping
the bad guys under lock and key.

Acknowledgment

I want to thank my husband's Cherokee cousins, Dee, Jack, Colleen, and Howard Ray, for helping me name Usdi, and for letting me be a part of the family for the past few decades.

Recognition also goes to my own brother and sister, Wolf and Paula, whose art celebrates our own Native American heritage. Thank you both for sharing the color, rhythm, and tradition of pow wows with me.

Chapter One

Hollow with longing, Jessica Holgrave leaned her forehead against the glass of the hospital nursery window. She wiped away a tear and watched as the baby's tiny pink face puckered in preparation to voice outrage at being wet, or hungry, or maybe just at being out in this cold, hard world.

Jessie wondered if she would ever find someone to love. Someone she could trust enough to share her life with. Someone to give her a child like the precious little bundle squirming on the other side of the glass wall.

"So, what do you think?"

Jessie turned to greet the new mother, her best

friend, with a hug. "You've done a wonderful job," she sighed. "She's just beautiful, Ellen."

"She is, isn't she?"

Jessie studied her friend's beaming face, then glanced away, looking again at the baby. It was wrong to be jealous of someone for whom she cared so deeply, but she couldn't help it. Ellen's joy only underscored the emptiness of her own personal life. Sure, she had friends and family, but no special someone. There had never been a special man in her life, not really. She'd begun to doubt there ever would be.

"Here, I brought her a little gift," she murmured, handing Ellen a gaily wrapped package.

"Oh boy, prezzies! Michelle just loves prezzies."

Jessie laughed. "And how could you possibly know that?"

"Because her mommy loves them, of course," Ellen declared smugly. "Come on back to my room and I'll open it."

Jessie shortened her steps to match Ellen's slow, shuffling gait, knowing what people saw when the two of them were together. A small, vivacious blond, Ellen Sanders stood a mere five foot two, with fluffy curls and big blue eyes. Her voice, high and almost child-like, perfectly complimented her dimpled smiles.

Jessie, on the other hand, loomed over her friend by a good eight inches. Ever since fifth grade, she'd been tall and gawky, teased about her height and taunted by classmates about her Cherokee heritage. Her body lines were long and lean, in direct contrast to Ellen's curvy proportions, and her straight black hair fell halfway down her back.

She and Ellen were opposite in temperament as well as looks. With her outgoing personality, Ellen made friends with everyone, while Jessie's reticence kept people at a distance. If Ellen hadn't blithely foisted her friendship upon Jessie when they were young girls, they wouldn't have this closeness now. It had never occurred to Ellen that Jessie might not want to be her friend. Jessie smiled to herself at the memory, thankful for Ellen's presence in her life.

"How are you feeling?" she asked Ellen.

"Like I've just had a baby."

"That doesn't tell me much."

"Your turn will come."

"I understand that the process takes two, a mother *and* a father? I'm afraid I don't see any candidates on the horizon."

Ellen giggled. "Oh, there're plenty of candidates for the siring part, every man you've ever met, probably." Jessie threw her a scowl. "But you're right, it takes a special man to fill the role of husband and father. He's out there somewhere, Jessie, just keep looking."

They reached Ellen's room. The new mother eased herself into a chair, motioning Jessie into another. "Let's see what we have here." She removed the wrapping paper and lifted the lid from the box. "Oh, Jessie, how perfect!"

The soft cloth doll had yellow yarn hair and a white dress printed all over with tiny pink rosebuds. Painted eyes and a shy smile made it the perfect first doll for any little girl. Ellen lifted it out of its tissue bed and smoothed back its hair, a pleased smile on her face.

"Hello, baby, how's my best girl?"

Both women looked up at the sound of a baritone voice; Ellen's face lighting to an adoring glow at the sight of her husband.

Jessie stood to greet him, and Mike put an arm around her shoulders. Plopping a brotherly kiss on her cheek he asked, "How ya doin', kid? Haven't seen you in ages."

"Fine, thanks." An arm around his waist, Jessie returned his hug. "Congratulations, Pop, that's some piece of work you two produced."

"How about that, isn't she great?"

A discreet cough from the doorway diverted Mike's attention. "Marsh, come on in." He motioned to the tall, broad-shouldered man filling the doorway. "Ladies, this is Marshall Abbott, the new kid on the block. Marsh, my wife, Ellen, and her best friend, Jessica Holgrave."

"A pleasure, Mrs. Sanders, Mrs. Holgrave."

"Miss Holgrave," Mike corrected.

Startled, Jessie found herself imprisoned by Marshall's forthright gaze. A voice as smooth as warmed honey flowed around her, then swirled through her blood. As he stepped into the room, Jessie could swear it diminished in size.

Sandy hair streaked by the sun fell in a wave over his tanned brow. Jessie tried to drag her eyes from his, but just then he smiled, a slow lifting of the lips, and her heart leaped against her ribs. His hazel irises warmed her insides before she finally broke the contact. Only then did she notice the distinctive badge pinned to his shirt. Disappointment slapped her like a wave of icy water.

What did you expect? He's the new man in Mike's unit. Of course he's a Ranger.

Marshall extended a box of chocolates to Ellen, along with a small gift-wrapped package for the baby.

"Oooh, more goodies, thank you," Ellen cooed. She unwrapped the candy, popped a chocolate creme into her mouth, then handed the box to Mike to pass around while she opened the baby's gift, a silver rattle on a mother-of-pearl teething ring. "How elegant! Look, Mike."

"Oh great. Thanks a lot, Abbott. You're setting a standard for my daughter that will take me two extra jobs to uphold."

Everyone laughed. Jessie had resumed her seat, but as Mike settled close to his wife and began to absently stroke her hair while telling her about his day, she felt like an interloper.

She glanced up and caught Marshall watching her. With a small nod towards the door, she asked, "Would you like to see the baby?"

"I guess I should. Mike may give me a quiz later."

The new parents laughed, and Mike answered, "I'll catch up with you in a minute."

Once in the corridor, Jess explained, "I thought they could use a little privacy." They reached the nursery and she pointed. "That's her, in the second row."

Only blond fuzz and pink blanket were visible until the nurse lifted the tiny bundle up to the glass for them to admire. The baby's eyes remained closed tightly in sleep, but she gnawed on one little fist, then yawned.

Marshall chuckled. "Cute as a pup."

The nurse tucked little Michelle back into her bassinet and Jessie turned toward the waiting room. He fell into step beside her. "So, have you known the Sanderses long?" he asked.

"Ellen and I have been friends since fourth grade. I've known Mike since high school."

They stopped in front of a soft drink machine. "What would you like?" Marshall asked.

"Root beer, please."

He handed her the can, then got himself a cola. "So you've known them for years and years then?"

She raised a gracefully arched brow at him. "What is it you want to know, Mr. Abbott?"

He grinned. "Not very subtle, huh?"

She shook her head slowly, her gaze locked with his.

"You're not married. Are you engaged?"

"No."

"Why not?"

Jessie choked on the sip she'd just taken. At least he had the good grace to look embarrassed. She turned to the utilitarian vinyl-covered furniture and took a seat, using the moment to regain her equilibrium.

"I'll bet you're a real popular guy, with a line like that."

"I'm sorry, I didn't mean to offend you." He eased down beside her on the plastic couch, stretching his legs out in front of him. "It just comes naturally to me."

"I'm not really offended. But you must admit, it's an unusual way to open a conversation."

"I guess." He studied the toes of his Western boots for a minute, then glanced sideways at her. "Look, I'm no good at small talk, and I'm curious about you. Any other vital statistics you'd be willing to divulge without me making a fool of myself first?"

"There's nothing interesting about me, but ask what you want and I'll answer."

"Seriously, you don't mind?"

"If you ask something I don't want you to know, I'll tell you so."

"Okay." He nodded and resumed his questioning. "So, you're not married or engaged. Are you seeing someone special?"

"No."

"Are you averse to dating?"

She shot him a scowl. "No, Mr. Abbott, I am not."

"Just making sure." He pulled himself upright, then rested his forearms on his thighs. "I once had a date with a woman who'd recently broken up with a cheating bum. The first time she saw me with someone else, she came after me with a butcher knife. After only one date, mind you!"

Jessie laughed. "I don't believe you."

"It's true. Honest, ask Mike."

The smile stayed in place as she squirmed into a more comfortable position on the sofa, turning partially toward him.

"Okay, on with the investigation. Any older brothers, or brothers at all who are bigger than me?"

Jessie thought about two of her older brothers. Jaquin, two years her senior, had defended her on playgrounds in the little oil towns they'd lived in as children, from Oklahoma to Texas. An East Texas sheriff had jailed Manny for punching out the drunk he'd found hassling her as she waited at the bus station for him to arrive home on leave. Both were sturdy men, but not nearly as tall as this Ranger.

"No."

"Great. How about dinner and a movie Saturday night?"

"I don't think so, but thank you."

"Why not?"

"I don't know you." She glanced away. He had a sense of humor, and she liked that, but she knew better than to trust the feeling of ease that was developing between them.

Her mother had often cautioned her against blithely trusting men she didn't know well, especially white men. An oilfield roughneck, Jessie's Caucasian father had adored his Native American wife. They'd met on a job site in Oklahoma, when she and her cousin came to sell fry bread and tacos for the men's lunch.

"But you must remember, not everyone is as

true of spirit as your father," she'd warn. Certainly Steve hadn't been. Nor the quarterback of the high school football team her senior year.

"Ah." Marshall interrupted her thoughts. "A cautious woman. Good for you. Mike will vouch for me," he coaxed.

"Somehow, I doubt that Mike has ever dated you." She cast him a quick glance.

"We work together. It's almost the same thing."

"Hardly."

"I could tell you about myself, and then you'd know me better."

"An unbiased opinion, naturally."

"Naturally," he agreed with a grin. "I'm thirty years old."

"Oh my, establishment age," she intoned dryly.

He gave her a mock scowl. "Don't interrupt. I've never been married, engaged once, two other serious girlfriends, none in the last three years. I'm six foot two inches, one hundred eighty-five pounds, and Protestant. I love hamburgers, hate spinach, have one sister and am of Scottish, English, and Italian extraction. I take my job seriously, but try to leave it behind at the end of the day. I'm dependable, honorable, and cats like me. So do most kids."

"Only most kids?"

"My sister's youngest squalls every time she sees me," he admitted.

Jessie chuckled in spite of herself. She liked a man who could make her laugh, but Marshall was still a lawman. She wasn't foolish enough to repeat her mistakes. Still, he was a friend of Mike's and she wanted to be polite.

"Tell you what," she offered. "I plan to take dinner to Mike and Ellen Saturday night. Why don't you join us?"

"I'd like that. I'll bring dessert. What time?"

Jessie left the small neighborhood hospital and headed north up Highway 249 through Tomball. She lived on the outskirts of the little Texas community nestled in an area of tall pines, ancient oaks, and family farms northwest of Houston.

The late spring air wafted through her open car window, heavy with the smell of newly mown grass. Along the roadside, pastel buttercups and vivid Mexican hats grew in colorful profusion.

She stopped at the barbecue hut and picked up some ribs for her supper. As she turned up the gravel lane that led to her modest brick home, she saw her black Chow waiting at the gate, his entire body wagging in greeting.

"Hey, boy, glad to see me?" Jessie greeted him as she crossed the yard. "Come on in and I'll feed you." She unlocked the door and held it for the dog, then fastened the screen behind her and went to the kitchen. A large silver tabby cat uncoiled herself from the sofa and silently followed them, sitting and waiting patiently while Jessie filled the dog's bowl before calling attention to herself with one loud meow.

Jessie reached down and scratched the cat under her chin. "What's the matter, Sheba, afraid I'd forget you? Not likely."

Jessie always talked out loud to her pets. If she didn't, she wouldn't have any conversation at all in the evenings.

The animals taken care of, she filled herself a plate and carried it into the living room to eat while she watched television.

After dinner, she washed her few dishes then took a shower and shampooed her hair. She sat on the corner of her bed to work out the tangles and think about Marshall Abbott. She often fantasized about having a man perform this chore for her. Strong hands gently easing a comb through the long tresses, a deep voice telling her how much he loved her.

Jessie sighed and gave herself a mental shake. *Come back to earth, Cinderella, there's no prince out there!* She turned her thoughts back to assessing the man she'd met this afternoon.

The job of a Texas Ranger could be dangerous,

but Marshall had the size for it. Not what she would call handsome, he was undeniably attractive in a rugged sort of way, with that shock of unruly hair and slumberous, expressive eyes. What color were they? Not dark. Gray maybe, or green. She couldn't remember.

Unfortunately, the man had the finesse of a runaway train. She shook her head. No man in his right mind asked a woman why she wasn't married, for Pete's sake!

She found it somehow endearing that he had, though, the childlike eagerness to make her acquaintance contrasting so starkly with his very adult size and age. And he'd looked so sincere, his gaze never wavering, while telling her about himself, as though he badly wanted her to find him acceptable.

What a laugh! *She* was the one who would fall short in the estimation of his family and friends. *Don't be a fool, Jessie. You don't really measure up in his book either. Remember Steve?*

She hadn't forgotten Steve. It simply wasn't possible. Her memory of the handsome deputy sheriff still had the power to shake her hard-won confidence in unguarded moments.

She'd met him at the intermediate school where she was a librarian. He had come to give a presentation on drugs to a student assembly. That weekend he'd called and asked her out.

She'd been bowled over by his golden hair and sky-blue eyes. His tailored uniform had accented the body of a god, and his handsome features caused women of all ages to stop and take a second look.

Don't go there. You don't want to dredge this up again! But her mind wouldn't cooperate. As though tired of being tamped down and relegated to a small dark corner, the memories unrolled like a strip of film. Her hand stilled, the comb falling to her lap.

She remembered her first few idyllic weeks with Steve. The way he made her laugh, his unflagging courtesy, the way he captured her heart.

The way he turned on her. The hateful things he'd said when she refused his advances, his features contorted in fury when she finally asked him to leave.

Two days later, he'd pulled her over as she was driving on a secluded stretch of road. He'd ordered her from the car and pinned her with his gaze. "What's the deal, Jessie?" he'd asked, hands propped on his black equipment belt. "You just playin' a game or something?"

She'd stood silent, not knowing what to say.

He'd shaken his head as though unable to understand. "A tall skinny thing like you can't get that many offers," he'd scoffed. "Well, I'm not offerin' again. You blew it, lady. I won't be back!"

A logging truck had come along the road just then, and he'd stepped back, allowing her to get into her car and drive away.

Hurt tightened her throat even now, and she looked down to discover the pain in her tightly curled fist came from the teeth of her forgotten comb.

No, she hadn't forgotten Steve, and, God help her, she'd never forget the lesson he'd taught her. No matter how pleasant Marshall Abbott's smiles, or how many times he made her laugh, come Saturday she'd be her polite, reserved self, then she'd never have to see the man again.

Saturday! She had to call Ellen and let her know that Marshall would be there too. Jessie reached for the phone.

"Hello?"

"Ellen, it's Jessie. I'm sorry to call so late."

Ellen laughed. "Late? Jessie, it's only eight o'clock."

"Oh. Anyway, I need to warn you. I invited Mike's friend Marshall over to have dinner with us Saturday. I hope it's okay."

"Of course, as long as everyone understands I'm not playing hostess. This kid eats every three hours, you know."

"That often? There's a lot about babies I don't know."

"You're a librarian, look it up," Ellen teased.

Jessie made a rude noise into the phone. "So you don't mind about Mr. Abbott?"

"Not at all, but I think he'd be hurt to hear you calling him Mr. Abbott. After you left, he grilled us unmercifully for information about you."

"He did?"

"Um hum. If I didn't know better, I'd think you were under investigation for a crime. The man's interested, Jessie."

"Big deal."

"Yeah? Then why did you invite him over Saturday?"

"Because he was pestering me to go out with him."

"See?"

"Like I said, big deal."

"It could be, if you're interested. Mike says he's a pretty nice guy. Give him a chance."

"I might. Just don't get your hopes up, El."

Chapter Two

Arriving at her usual early hour before the school bell rang, Jessie found a dark-eyed boy in neatly patched jeans and a faded shirt waiting for her.

"Good morning, Billy."

"Mornin', Miss Holgrave."

Jessie unlocked the library door. "What can I do for you?"

The boy hesitantly handed her a book, the back cover half torn off. "My baby sister got hold of it. Ma says I'll have to find some way to pay you."

Jessie took the book and examined it carefully. "I see." She turned the volume over and ran a hand across it as she continued to inspect the damage.

The boy stood straight and quiet, prepared to take responsibility. No excuses for his careless-ness, no pleading that he didn't have the money to pay for it.

Jessie knew his family. Dirt-poor, but honest to the bone. They refused to apply for any kind of assistance, making do instead on what they could earn, instilling in their children respect, pride, and responsibility. It was too bad more people weren't like that.

"You're in what, seventh grade now, Billy?"

"Yes, ma'am."

"Let me talk to Mr. Meyers. I can fix this, but it won't be quite as good as before. Maybe he'll let you work it off after school by helping weed the flower bed around the flagpole."

"Yes, ma'am. I'm sorry, Miss Holgrave, I won't take any more books home."

"Now, just a minute, young man, that's not what this is about." Jessie touched his shoulder. "I want you to check books out. Just be sure to keep them zipped in your backpack when you're not reading them, okay?"

Billy grinned, his brown eyes shining. "Yes, ma'am!"

Jessie flipped on the rest of the lights and opened the blinds. Students drifted in, dropping off books in the return box, some going to the shelves to find new ones.

Checking her schedule, Jessie saw that Pam Mellor's eighth grade class would be in during second period to do research for their English report. Pete Wade had his science class scheduled for fourth period. Jessie sighed. Pete always tried to hit on her while his kids ran roughshod over the library. Maybe she could arrange to have Mr. Meyers meet with her here that period on the matter of Billy Stovall.

Spaghetti and a garden salad didn't constitute a very fancy dinner, but could be transported easily. Jessie added a pint of cherry tomatoes, then snapped the lid on a big plastic bowl. Which dressing to take? Italian, of course. She dropped a bottle into the bag with the garlic bread and wine. What else? Oh, Parmesan cheese. She rummaged in her refrigerator until she found it, adding the canister to the grocery bag. All set.

Carefully loading everything into her car, Jessie tried hard to ignore her mounting nervousness. After all, she had no reason to be nervous. She was just taking dinner to her best friend's house. Of course, Marshall Abbott would be there too, if he hadn't forgotten. No, she really didn't think he'd forget. Thus, the nerves.

She cranked the car's air conditioner up full

blast to keep the salad from wilting before she got to Ellen's. It was only late April, but the temperature had already hit the mid-eighties.

At the stoplight in Tomball where the highway intersected with the small town's main street, a pickup truck full of young men drew up beside her. Radio blaring, the boys in the truck bed were being loud and rowdy, jostling each other and cutting up. "Hey," one of them yelled, "it's Miss Holgrave."

The others all turned, whistling and calling out. A couple of them hung over the side of the truck to peer into her window.

"Howdy, Miss Holgrave, where ya going?"

"How about giving me a ride, Miss Holgrave?"

Jessie waved, then tried to ignore them. They were all high school students; several had been at her middle school only a couple of years ago. They were probably in the area stirring up mischief for their rivals at the Tomball school. The truck's driver began blowing the horn to get her attention. A passenger in the cab leaned out the window and yelled, "Hey, Miss Holgrave! Lookin' good!"

The light turned green and Jessie left the intersection with a small squeal of tires. The boys came after her, laying down a good amount of rubber in the process. Jessie glanced in her rearview mirror. Naturally, you couldn't find a cop when you wanted one.

Heading southbound on the highway, she picked up speed as she cleared town, slipping through traffic. The truck kept her in sight, giving her cause to be concerned for the boys riding in the back. Not so concerned that she would let them catch up to her, though.

A dozen rowdy teenagers did not present a pleasant scenario. Taken singly, she wouldn't fear a one of those boys, but that had nothing to do with the current situation. Not that she was really frightened of them. She just didn't see any reason to take chances. At the next major intersection, she left the highway, hoping she could disappear into Ellen's neighborhood before the boys saw her.

The subdivision's entrance was a block ahead; Jessie heard the truck's horn behind her as the boys made the turn. Though nearly to her destination, she hated the idea that they would make a scene in front of Ellen's, possibly upsetting her and the baby. She pulled her car into the driveway and got out. A moment later, the truck blocked the end of the drive, and two of the youths vaulted over the side and quickly cut her off.

"Miss Holgrave, that's not very neighborly, trying to lose us like that," one boy scolded.

"What the devil is going on out here?" Mike appeared and came striding across the yard, Marshall at his side. "Are you all right, Jessie?"

"Let's get outta here," one boy yelled as he dove back into the truck. The others scrambled down low in the bed. The driver muttered an oath and dropped the vehicle into first, grinding the gears in his haste to flee.

Mike spun on his heel, ordering Marshall over his shoulder, "See about Jessie while I make the call."

With two more long strides, Marshall reached her and grasped her arms. "Are you okay?"

"I'm fine, really." Jessie turned away, freeing herself from his light grip. "Just a bunch of kids with spring fever."

"More like buck fever," he muttered. He reached for the grocery bag she'd lifted from the back seat. "Let me help you carry this stuff in."

"Thanks." She retrieved the salad. "I'll get the doors."

When they entered the house, she overheard Mike on the phone. "Yeah, that's right, John. Pike Swartz's kid. They're in the boy's truck and they're out raising a little Cain. About five minutes ago. Good. Thanks, buddy."

He hung up and turned to the room with a smile. "The sheriff's boys should be able to find them. If I know Pike, he'll take the keys away, just because the boy interrupted his own party-ing."

"Why were they after you?"

Jessie glanced up at Marshall's puzzled question and shrugged. "Nothing better to do, I guess. Let's get this food into the kitchen."

Marshall followed, but wouldn't let the matter drop. "Is this one of those things you don't want to tell me?"

Jessie avoided looking at him as she got the food ready to serve. "Not really. It's one of those things I shouldn't have to tell you."

Marshall planted himself in the middle of the floor, arms crossed over his chest. "What does that mean?"

Jessie stopped her work and looked at him in exasperation. "Where are you from?"

"I was born over by Fort Worth. Why?"

"So you're a native Texan?"

"Yes. But what . . ."

"And you're a law officer."

"Yes, I've just been taken into the Rangers from the Texas Highway Patrol. Exactly where is this leading?"

"To your answer. As a highway patrolman, you may have been fairly democratic. Even as a na-tive son of, what was it, Irish and English extraction, you may have harbored few prejudices. But I doubt your generous attitude will last too much longer."

"My forefathers were Scottish, English, and Italian," he corrected, "but I still fail to see what you're getting at."

Jessie studied him a minute, this tall man planted stubbornly in the middle of Ellen's kitchen, brows drawn down over hazel eyes. Hazel. That's why she couldn't remember. They were neither brown nor green, but both.

"I'm waiting," Marshall reminded her.

Jessie shrugged and tried to sound nonchalant. "Your forefathers were primarily European, mine weren't."

"Obviously."

Jessie abandoned her calm façade, snapping, "Yes, obviously, and there you have your answer. There are still plenty of people around here, mostly male I might add, from otherwise polite families who believe that dark-skinned women were born to be hassled. Now do you understand?"

The woman was magnificent! Fists planted on her hips, her color heightened by annoyance, she faced him squarely. Her eyes snapped sparks and her breath hissed from between clenched teeth. Marshall had an almost undeniable urge to grab her and kiss her senseless, and heritage had nothing to do with it. Instead, he shook his head to clear it, then said with amazement, "You're kidding!"

Jessie snorted in contempt. "Like this is all news to you, right?"

She turned back to the counter and began to vigorously toss the salad. A fight over prejudice and racial discrimination wasn't what she'd imagined for this afternoon's conversation. Darn those boys! Why couldn't they have headed the other direction in their search for fun instead of going up to Tomball?

Oh well, it would have come up sooner or later. It always did. When the men she knew were ready to marry, they chose nice white girls for their brides.

"Have you always been a bigot?"

Her head snapped up. Marshall leaned one hip against the sink beside her, his arms still crossed, wearing an expression of bland curiosity.

"I beg your pardon?"

"Have you always been a bigot?" he repeated politely.

"Where did you . . ."

"You assume Caucasian native Texans are prejudiced, as well as most lawmen. That sounds like bigotry to me."

Jessie waved her hand dismissively. "You don't—"

"What about Mike?" Marshall interrupted. "He's been a Ranger for three years. Do you tolerate his attitude just for Ellen's sake?"

"Mike doesn't have an attitude," Jessie growled.

"Ah, but you said—"

Jessie took a turn at interrupting. "Let's just drop it, okay? This is supposed to be a celebration for Mike and Ellen."

After a moment's silence, Marshall agreed. "Truce. Do I have to smoke a pipe or something?"

Jessie turned on him in fury, but he grinned down at her so disarmingly she couldn't help chuckling. "Keep that up and you're liable to lose your scalp before the evening's out."

Marshall bit back a smart retort and simply smiled. He'd learned more about her in the last few minutes than he had from all the questions he'd asked yesterday. And his scalp was the least of his worries.

Jessie wiped off the countertops and rinsed out the dishrag. She'd been quiet during dinner, letting the others do most of the talking while she made sure everyone had plenty to eat. The men were outside now, Mike showing Marshall the deck he'd just built. Ellen had taken Michelle into the bedroom to nurse.

Jessie plugged in the coffee pot, then put fat wedges of the carrot cake Marshall had brought on saucers for the men, slicing more modest pieces for Ellen and herself. Normal, routine activities, but they made her feel like part of a family.

A moment later, she paused at Ellen's bedroom door. "Hi. Want some company?"

Ellen smiled. "Come on in and sit down." She lay across the bed, her baby snuggled against her breast. "This little chowhound is on her second course already."

As if in answer, Michelle wiggled and began sucking noisily.

"What a little piggy," Jessie observed.

Someone tapped gently on the door, and Jessie stood. "Sounds like Daddy wants to join the party. There's coffee and cake whenever you're ready."

She stepped into the hall and found Mike balancing his cake on top of a cup of coffee. He grinned at her. "Don't worry, I'll share."

"See that you do. It isn't polite to eat in front of others," Jessie scolded in her best librarian's voice.

Back in the kitchen, she found Marshall pouring himself a cup of coffee. He glanced up, then took another cup from the shelf and filled it.

"Thank you."

"My pleasure. Do you want to take your cake outside? It's really nice now that the sun's down."

"Okay. We can break in Mike's new deck."

As Mike had, Marshall balanced his saucer of cake on the top of his coffee cup and opened the sliding glass door, then closed it behind them. Jessie took a seat in one of the cushioned lawn chairs and set her coffee on a small redwood table. Marshall took a seat facing her.

A soft breeze stirred the scents of newly blossomed flowers and freshly dug earth. "It is nice out here," Jessie conceded, as if there'd been a difference of opinion.

"I wouldn't lie to you."

Marshall's tone insinuated he meant more than the obvious. "Why did you say that?"

"Just so you know."

Her eyes met his direct gaze a minute longer, then retreated to the saucer in her lap. She took a bite of cake. "Mmm, this is good. Where did you get it?"

"Why do you think I didn't make it?"

Jessie arched one eyebrow at him in a give-me-a-break look and he started laughing. "Okay, I said I wouldn't lie. I didn't say I wouldn't tease." His eyes continued to sparkle at her over his cup as he took a sip. "There's a great little sandwich and pastry shop around the corner from my condo. They do a good job, huh?"

Her mouth full, Jessie could only nod.

"I'd be glad to show you where it is."

She followed the cake with a swallow of coffee before asking, "The pastry shop or your condo?"

"Both."

"Thanks, but I think I'll pass."

"On my condo or the pastry shop?"

"Both."

Marshall chuckled. "Well, at least I know it's nothing personal. You couldn't have anything against the pastry shop."

Jessie relaxed enough to allow a fleeting smile.

"You have a nice smile. I wish you'd use it more often."

What did one answer to something like that?

"You also have a nice voice that I'd like to hear more of."

She set her plate aside and met his gaze head on. "I thought you said you weren't good at small talk," she challenged.

He shrugged. "They say necessity is the mother of invention, and you won't talk, so it's necessary for me to if I want to get to know you."

"I thought we'd already taken care of that."

"How so?"

"I told you in no uncertain terms where I'm

coming from when I first got here this evening. The matter doesn't usually come up quite so soon, but that truckload of boys helped clear the air, don't you think?"

"Jess, have a heart. I'm just a small-town boy myself, with a simple Bachelor's degree, so if you're going to mess with my mind, provide the footnotes."

She did have a heart, and it skipped a beat when he called her "Jess" that way. Though she had little doubt he understood her perfectly, Jessie gave him a succinct explanation.

"I don't play house."

Marshall leaned an elbow on his chair and propped his chin on his fist. For several long minutes he met her glare with a forthright gaze. Finally, he shook his head. "You know," he said, totally without humor, "this is the first time I can remember being turned down before I even thought about asking."

Jessie's mouth fell open and her face flooded with heat. Talk about being neatly put in your place! She snapped her jaw closed and shot to her feet, escape the only thought on her mind.

Marshall moved quickly for such a large man. He was on his feet and blocking her path before she could reach the door. Jessie couldn't meet his eyes, so she stared mutely at his throat, concentrating on the pulse beating in its hollow.

"Come on, Jess," he said quietly, grasping her fingers, "give me a chance."

With a light touch, he lifted her chin, but she stubbornly refused to meet his gaze. "Please?"

She already knew the man well enough to realize he wouldn't let it go. She'd have to respond. "I . . . I don't understand. What do you want from me?"

"Not much for now. A smile, a little conversation, preferably without blame and accusations, and some time to spend with you."

He seemed like such a gentle man, his touch light, his eyes tender, his voice low and soothing. Jessie's gaze rested on his unsmiling lips. Would they be gentle as well? Would his kiss be tender? Reluctantly, she raised her eyes. "And later?"

He took a step back. "That will be entirely up to you."

Jessie glanced down at her hands, twisted together nervously. "All right," she murmured and slowly returned to her seat.

The back door slid open and Mike called over his shoulder to Ellen, "Here they are, on the deck. I've got the cake, bring the coffee."

Jessie jumped up to help Ellen, grateful for the interruption. They all had another slice of cake and more coffee. For the next hour and a half, the conversation covered a variety of unrelated subjects ranging from Michelle to the possible work assignments of a Texas Ranger in a metropolis like Houston.

When Ellen went in to check on the baby for the third time, Jessie joined her. They found Michelle awake, so after changing her Ellen laid the infant in Jessie's arms.

"It's a good fit," Ellen noted. "You should get one of your own."

"You're beginning to sound like my mother."

"I just want you to be as happy as I am. How is Raquel?"

"Okay, I guess. She doesn't seem to be as strong as before the pneumonia, though, and it worries me."

"How old is she now?"

"Sixty-four. Not really all that old."

"But she had eight children, Jessie, and a pretty sparse life before she married your father. All that takes its toll on a person's health."

"I know. That's why I'm worried."

As they talked, Jessie instinctively rocked Michelle in her arms, absorbing the feel of the warm little body flexing and burrowing against her. The infant began to fuss, and Jessie transferred her to her shoulder, stroking the small silky head with her cheek and murmuring nonsense. The baby quieted for awhile, but then began fussing in earnest.

"Time to eat again," Ellen explained as she reached for her daughter.

Jessie kissed the furrowed little brow before handing Michelle over. "See you later, dumpling." To Ellen, she said, "I'd better be getting home. I'll call you tomorrow."

Ellen hugged her with one arm. "Thanks for the dinner and the company. We really appreciate it."

"Glad to do it. Call me if you need anything."

The men came in from the yard as Jessie gathered up her dishes. "Leaving already?" Mike asked.

"You and Ellen are both exhausted, and don't try to tell me otherwise. I'll see you again soon, don't worry."

Mike laughed and gave her a peck on the cheek. "Thanks for dinner, kid, you saved her from my Omelet a la Mike."

"I'm going now too, Mike. Thanks for having me." The men shook hands, then Marshall took the sack of kitchenware from Jessie, telling her, "I'll follow you home."

"You will not."

"Look, if the location of your residence is a closely guarded secret, you can dump me at the last major intersection, but I want to make sure that truckload of junior cowboys isn't lurking around somewhere."

"He's right, Jessie," Mike added, "Ricky may have eluded John's men. I don't want you taking any chances."

Jessie crossed her arms stubbornly. "This is ridiculous! I'm an adult and have been taking care of myself for a long time. Besides, those boys are probably all home where they belong by now."

"Okay, have it your way," Mike sighed. Marshall started to protest, but Mike stayed him with a raised palm. "It doesn't do any good to argue with her, Marsh. I'll see that she gets home okay."

"Mike, I will not let you leave Ellen alone," Jessie argued.

"It'll only be for an hour. Besides, Ellen would want me to go and you know it."

"No."

"You can't stop me, Jessie," he pointed out.

"Oh, all right," she huffed, "he can come."

Mike nodded. "Leave her at the second traffic light after the highway intersects with Tomball's main street," he instructed. "She'll be a half mile from home there. But, Jessie, you call as soon as you're in the door so I won't worry."

"For Pete's sake," she grumbled.

"Jessie?"

"Okay, okay."

If not for her stubborn streak, Jessie might have admitted that it felt nice having someone look out for her. But she couldn't. She refused to acknowledge the fancy Jeep in her rearview mirror. Only as she left the highway did she look to see him turning around to go back the way he'd come. She wondered fleetingly how far out of his way Marshall had traveled to see her safely home.

No black pickup truck lurked on this street, and as she turned up her own graveled lane, she quickly confirmed that nothing waited there, either. She called Mike as promised, then took a long, leisurely shower. During the night, a tall man with a Ranger's badge pinned to his shirt strolled through her dreams.

Chapter Three

Jessie sat on the porch eating a sandwich, the Chow in front of her watching closely for any dropped morsels. "Nan, you're such a beggar. You act like I never feed you," she scolded. The dog cocked his head to one side and gave his tightly curled tail a single wag.

She heard the telephone peal through the screen door. Jessie got up and tossed the remaining corner of her lunch to the waiting dog.

"Hello?"

"Hello, Miss Holgrave, this is Marsh Abbott. Lovely afternoon, isn't it?"

"How did you get my number?"

"It's in the telephone book."

"Oh." She mentally slapped her forehead. *Duh.*

"I'd like to see you today. Would you meet me somewhere?"

"Like where?"

"How about over by Willowbrook Mall? We could take in a movie, then go to dinner, unless you'd prefer something more active. In which case I could meet you at Celebration Station by the freeway and we could shoot some miniature golf and ride the go-carts."

"Either one sounds fine."

"Such enthusiasm, Miss Holgrave. I'm going to have to give my ego a good pep talk before I leave the house."

"This is your idea, Mr. Abbott."

Marshall sighed dramatically. "Fair enough. Since the day's half gone, let's do a movie and dinner. We'll save the fun and games for a full day's outing."

"Aren't you getting ahead of yourself?"

"Not really. I'm just trying to reinflate my punctured self-esteem."

Jessie smiled. "What time?"

She heard paper rustling as Marshall consulted the theater listings. "Let's see, the new Tom Cruise movie starts again in forty-five minutes, or we have Costner in an hour and a half. Which is better for you?"

"I've been weeding flower beds, so Kevin Costner would give me the time I need to clean up."

"Costner it is, then. I'll wait for you by the theater entrance. Unless you'd rather I pick you up?"

"No, I'll meet you."

Marshall laughed. "I thought so. Thanks, Jess, I'll be waiting."

Jessie hung up, shaking her head, a bemused smile on her face. The man was pushy, but, then again, not really. He'd insisted on seeing her home last night, but left her short of her destination as requested. He wanted to see her again today, but accepted that she preferred to meet him. Glancing at the clock, she jumped up and closed the front door, then headed to the shower.

Half an hour later, Jessie struggled with getting a comb through her wet hair. Someday she'd give up and just cut it all off! Her mind skipped on. What would she wear? She didn't want it to appear as if she'd tried to impress him.

Jeans. Jeans and what? A sweater? No. A blouse or shirt? Most of her blouses would look silly with jeans, and she didn't want to be insultingly casual. After all, she'd agreed to this date. Jessie snapped her fingers. She had the perfect shirt: a royal blue sueded silk that she hadn't even had the chance to wear yet.

She spent another five minutes trying to decide whether to tuck it in or leave it out and cinch it with a belt. In the end, she tucked it in and rolled the sleeves up a couple of turns. She twisted her hair into a coil and secured it with large silver pins.

A dash of perfume, a dab of lipstick, grab her purse and keys. On the front porch she stopped. Forgot earrings. Jessie grabbed the first silver pair she found and pushed them through her ears while she walked. Back on the porch, she checked to make sure she had her keys before locking the door. This wouldn't be a good time to lock herself out of the house.

Keys in hand, she paused to take a deep breath. *Okay, Jessie, this is it. Ready or not, here you go.* She hated that thoughts of Marshall made her so nervous.

Jessie cruised the crowded parking lot around the theater until she finally spotted an open space. She pulled in, killed the engine, then checked her hair and makeup in the mirror. She reached for her purse with her right hand as she opened the car door with her left, bumping someone in the process.

"Oh, I'm sorry!"

"That's okay," Marshall answered as he turned around, offering a hand to help her out. When

Jessie straightened, he perused her quickly and added, "The pleasure is definitely worth the pain."

Jessie frowned, and he amended, "Too flowery? How about, you look great?"

Jessie accepted the compliment grudgingly. "Thanks."

Marshall took her arm and carefully steered her across the asphalt, winding through parked cars and watching the traffic.

At the movie theater, he bought them soft drinks and a huge tub of buttered popcorn, then tried to figure out how to carry it all. Jessie watched him struggle for a minute before stepping forward to help. "You're really going overboard trying to prove you're a gentleman," she teased. "Let me carry the popcorn and you can slosh our drinks."

"You, Jess Holgrave, are a hard woman," he grouched.

Jessie chuckled, then asked over her shoulder, "Do you really think so?"

The answer came from close behind her right ear, so close she could feel the heat of his breath when he murmured, "No, I really think you're just scared."

A tremor shot through her body all the way to her toes. He was absolutely right, of course, but it unnerved her that he'd guessed.

She chose their seats, and Marshall settled beside her, helping Jessie wedge the popcorn between them. When he draped his arm across the back of her chair, she raised an eyebrow in his direction. Marshall tilted his head back and laughed softly.

"Come on, Jess, you can't mean to be that puritanical. I'm doing my best, can't you give just a little?"

Jessie didn't answer, merely rolling her eyes heavenward and shaking her head. Marshall chuckled and squeezed her shoulders. "That's my girl."

"Don't push it," Jessie grumped.

"A man can dream, can't he?"

Jessie gave up and feigned interest in the previews on screen. However, the warmth and solidity of the arm bracketing her shoulders didn't escape her notice. At some point during the movie, Marshall began to lightly caress her upper arm with his fingertips, rubbing them lightly up and down her brushed silk sleeve. Jessie shifted in the seat, relaxing against him a little.

Outside the theater, Marshall stretched his arms over his head, then flexed his shoulders. "Where shall we eat? We have a choice of the two leading fast-food burger chains, one of the pizza chains, two Italian restaurants, one barbecue house, and a gourmet hamburger emporium. Or we could go to the mall food court. No, scratch that. We could go across the way to a Mexican restaurant."

"I'll let you choose. I chose the movie."

Marshall grinned at her. "Brave girl. Okay, how about one of the Italian restaurants?"

"Which one?"

"The one with the fewest cars around it."

Jessie laughed, and Marshall basked in it. He wondered what it would take to keep her laughing all the time.

Again, Jessie had no more than turned off her engine before Marshall waited to open her door. She accepted his hand more easily this time, flashing him a quick self-conscious smile.

The smile faded, and Marshall's gaze flitted from Jessie's lips to her hair. He lifted a hand to the back of her head then paused. "Would you mind?" he asked softly.

Her eyes widened momentarily just before a blush climbed her cheeks. Jessie dropped her gaze and gave a small shake of her head. She heard him exhale and realized he'd been holding his breath.

Marshall gently removed the big pins that held her coiled hair in place and watched in fascination as the heavy mass cascaded down her back. He brushed the stray strands back over her shoulder and handed her the pins.

Jessie stood absolutely still, her body so attuned to him it very nearly vibrated. He met her eyes again, and said simply, "Thank you."

"Jess?"

She looked up. "What?"

"Are you ready to order?"

Still shaken by the incident in the parking lot, Jessie couldn't seem to concentrate. "Yes, of course. Iced tea, please."

"We have our drinks, Jess," Marshall pointed out gently. "What would you like to eat?"

"I don't know," she murmured. "Whatever you're having is fine."

Marshall reached across the table and laid his hand over hers. "Are you okay?"

Embarrassed by her confusion, she blustered, "Of course I am. Just order for me, would you?"

He drew back. "Whatever the lady wants. We'll have two orders of the veal scaloppine, and bring the fried vegetable plate for an appetizer."

The waiter bowed and departed, restoring some measure of privacy. Jessie could feel Marshall's gaze, and began to flush again under his scrutiny.

"I've never seen hair so black. The light reflects off it like off a crow's wing, almost blue."

Jessie couldn't remember being at such a loss for words as she was when in this man's company. Usually she remained silent simply by choice.

Marshall reached for her hand, picking it up and rubbing his thumb across the back. "I'm sorry, Jess, I don't mean to make you uncomfortable."

"Be that as it may . . ." She left the thought unfinished.

Marshall squeezed her hand and released it. "Okay, I'll back off." He tilted his head and grinned at her. "Besides, I wouldn't want you running for cover. It's too hard coaxing you out as it is."

"Good idea. Keep that in mind."

After that, she relaxed and enjoyed his company, asking what he expected to be doing in his new job.

"Well, in the two and a half months I've been here, I've been trying to crack a coyote's pipeline."

Jessie raised an eyebrow and pierced him with a hard look.

"A coyote is a human predator who victimizes illegal aliens, charging them exorbitant fees to smuggle them into this country. An experience many of them don't survive, by the way."

"I know what a coyote is," Jessie replied coolly.

"Oh. You think the term is derogatory, then."

She didn't answer.

"It's no different than loan shark, or drug lord.

In my opinion, it's a pretty benign term for someone low enough to pack three dozen men into the
back of a moving van last summer, lock the door
from the outside, and send them across the state
in blistering heat with no ventilation and no water. Half the men died before the truck was
stopped in Austin. Three more died in the hospital."

Jessie braced an elbow on the table and studied
his face, her chin resting on her hand. Marshall's
anger on behalf of the victimized immigrants
seemed genuine enough. Maybe she did have a
chip on her shoulder. "Point conceded."

"Thank you. Now what about you? Ellen said
you're a librarian?"

"I'm employed by the Cypress Valley School
District. I'm the librarian at Wannamaker Middle
School."

"So those boys the other night . . ."

Jessie nodded. "Some of them were former students of mine."

"Other than keeping the bookshelves straight,
what does a school librarian do?"

"I teach the kids how to use the library and
help them find research material. I mend damaged
books, order special materials for the teachers,
recommend acquisitions to the school board, that
sort of thing."

"Do you like your job?"

"Very much."

"Why?"

Jessie paused to consider her answer. Behind Marshall's country-boy façade lay a shrewd mind. "I like my job because," she began in grade-school report fashion, "I like kids and because it's not socially intensive."

"You mean, as in adult population."

"That's right. Up until their last semester in middle school, most children are pleasant enough people to work with."

"What happens that last semester?"

"Their hormones kick in and they mutate."

Marshall laughed, then looked at her curiously. "But even then, they're still better than their adult counterparts?"

"That's it," Jessie confirmed.

"Have you always been so antisocial?" he teased.

"I suppose, though I think of it more as being introverted than antisocial."

"I wouldn't call anyone with a temper like yours an introvert."

Marshall grinned at her, and Jessie blushed. "I'm usually very mild-mannered, unless cornered."

"Oh? Interesting."

Uncomfortable with the drift of their conversation, Jessie attempted to redirect it. "Why would a ranger from the Houston office be assigned to track a, ah, coyote? I'd think someone stationed closer to the border would get that job."

Astute hazel eyes assessed Jessie for a moment, then Marshall shrugged, letting her have her way. "Normally, that might be the case, but we believe this man is headquartered here in the Houston area. We're not as interested in his hired hands as we are in nailing him."

Jessie studied the man seated across from her while he described the tactics he would use to apprehend the mastermind behind the alien smuggling operation. Marshall's expression became intense, but his voice remained flat as he related scenarios of failed attempts, dead ends, and his struggles with his mounting frustration. His hazel eyes darkened, and he unconsciously balled his hands into fists beside his plate. She could see how important his job was to him, and how badly he wanted to bring this vile opportunist to justice.

Watching him, Jessie softened a little. His determination to avenge the criminal's victims and to protect future unfortunates from falling prey to the coyote touched her, and she could tell she was lowering her defenses just a bit.

Marshall abruptly fell silent, aware of how caught up he'd become in his narrative. His cheeks warmed and he shot Jessie a sheepish grin. "Sorry, I guess I got a little carried away."

She gave him one of her rare smiles. "Not at all. It's refreshing to listen to someone who still champions truth, justice, and the American way."

For a change, Marshall found himself speechless. Her approval swelled somewhere in his chest, like a sunflower lifting its face to the light. And that smile! Lord, would you look at that smile! He reached across the table and took her hand.

"Did you know you're very easy to talk to?"

Jessie shrugged self-consciously. "I guess it's because I don't usually say a whole lot myself."

"Maybe, but I think it's because you appear to really be interested in what I'm saying."

"I am."

"Why?"

Because I'm interested in you. "Well, we tend to think of the Texas Rangers as a part of history. We don't hear much about what they do today, and it's intriguing to hear about the modern-day cases and methods."

Much to Jessie's relief, Marshall accepted that at face value. She gently withdrew her hand from his on the pretext of picking up her glass.

Marshall smiled knowingly and returned his attention to his meal. They finished in companionable silence, and he ushered Jessie to her car, took her keys to unlock the door, and held it open for her. She slid into the seat and held her hand out for the keys, but Marshall stepped into the space beside her and dropped to a crouch, bringing their eyes to a level.

"Jess, thank you for meeting me. I've really enjoyed being with you these past two days."

He spoke in low, husky tones, and the hairs on Jessie's arms prickled. She bit her lower lip and he dropped his eyes to the keys he tossed in one hand.

"I guess you need these, huh?"

Jessie nodded. Marshall's empty hand reached for hers. Cupping it palm up, he gently laid the keys in the center and folded her fingers over them with his other hand. They remained motionless like that, Jessie seated in her car, Marshall crouched beside her, her hand cradled between his wide palms, their eyes fixed on their joined hands.

Finally, Marshall sighed. "I don't want you to leave."

Jessie met his gaze. "I know," she whispered.

"Can I call you?"

A small grin tugged at one corner of Jessie's mouth as she answered, correcting his grammar in the process, "Yes, you may."

Marshall's eyes twinkled in response. "Thank you, teacher."

Jessie started the car. Marshall straightened beside her. When she reached to pull her door shut she looked up, waiting for him to step back. Instead, he bent and touched her lips in a fleeting kiss, then stepped quickly back and shut her door.

Twenty minutes later, Jessie was surprised to find herself sitting in the car in front of her house. She didn't remember anything about the drive home.

Chapter Four

On Tuesday afternoon, Jessie's phone rang five minutes after she'd come in the door.

Ellen didn't bother with a salutation. "Well, you've made a conquest."

"Ellen?"

"Who else?"

"Hello to you too. Now what in the world are you babbling about?"

"As if you didn't know! This has to be a record, even for you. Come on, Jessie, give me the details."

"Ellen Elizabeth, if you don't calm down this minute and tell me what the devil you're talking about, I'm going to call Mike and tell him you've flipped out."

Ellen heaved an impatient sigh. "I'm talking about Marshall Abbott, the latest man to fall head over heels for you. Now tell me how you accomplished it so quickly, and don't leave out a single juicy tidbit."

"For heaven's sake, I just met the man for dinner and a movie, that's all. Afterwards I drove home and I suppose he did too."

"You didn't even let him come in?"

"We parted ways at the restaurant, Ellen. At the mall. He called and asked if I'd meet him there for a movie and dinner."

"Must have been some movie," Ellen muttered, disappointed at the lack of drama.

Jessie laughed. "Well, Kevin Costner is pretty easy on the eyes," she teased.

"Jessica Bluefeather Holgrave!"

Like a family member, Ellen only used Jessie's full name when thoroughly upset with her.

"Ellen, calm down," Jessie soothed, "or you're going to curdle your milk."

That brought an involuntary chuckle from her friend. "Well, can you blame me? According to Mike, Marshall Abbott spent the entire day yesterday talking about you, obviously far gone. And when I call you for the lowdown, what do I get: 'Oh, we went to dinner and a movie, that's all.' We used to confide in each other, Jessie."

"Honest, that's about it, El." Ellen didn't respond and Jessie sighed. Sensitive to the hurt she'd heard in her friend's voice she confessed, "He did ask if he might call me and I said yes." Ellen snorted. "And he kissed me just before I left."

"All right, that's more like it!"

"Ellen," Jessie cautioned, "it was just a quick light friendly-type kiss."

"Tell that to Marshall. I'm serious, Jessie, this man is hot on your trail."

"I believe 'hot' is the operative word here, Ellen, and what's new about that?"

"I don't think he's that kind, Jessie, I really don't."

"Maybe not. We'll see."

"Then you *are* going to go out with him again?"

"Probably."

"That's better." Ellen's voice was smug. "Keep me posted."

Jessie emerged from the bathroom wrapped in a terry robe, pulling the pins from her coiled hair. She reached for her hairbrush just as the telephone rang. Absently pulling the bristles through the thick strands, she reached for the receiver.

"Hello?"

"Hello, this is Marsh. Am I interrupting anything?"

Jessie answered, "No, I'm ah, doing my hair."

"Doing your hair?"

"Yes."

"What are you 'doing' to it?"

"Just brushing it out."

"Ah." Marsh pictured her pulling a brush through that magnificent ebony mane. In order for her to reach the ends she would have to pull it over one shoulder. He swallowed. "That's, ah, that's nice. How was your day?"

"Pretty good. How about yours?"

"Not too bad."

"Any more leads?"

"Not really."

"I'm sorry."

"Yeah, me too. But something's bound to come up. The crops are nearly ready for harvesting, so he'll be stepping up his operations. Not only does he get money from the laborers, but some of the growers pay him a bonus for bringing in cheap help."

"Sounds lucrative."

"Of course it is. Why do you think he goes to so much trouble?"

Jessie had no response.

"Listen, I just called to tell you how much I enjoyed Sunday."

"Thank you, so did I."

"Really, Jess?"

There it was again, the childlike appeal for approval, the intimate abbreviation of her name. "Yes, Marshall, really."

"Would you be willing to try it again?"

Jessie laughed. "That depends what you have in mind."

"Do you ride?"

"Ride?"

"Horseback."

"Was Custer a white man?"

Marshall laughed. "How about I pick you up, or meet you," he corrected, "Friday afternoon. What time do you get home from school?"

"About three-thirty. Where are we going?"

"A friend of mine has a place not far from you. He trains quarter horses for ranch work and keeps mine for me."

"You have your own horse?"

"Yes, ma'am, ah shore do," Marshall drawled teasingly, "got me my own gun, an' boots, too. But shucks, ain't nuthin', jest reg'ler Ranger gear, iffn ya know what ah mean."

Jessie's laughter poured through the line, igniting a fizzle in Marshall's chest and painting his face with a wide smile.

"That's awful," she chortled.

"What's so awful about having a horse?"

"Not the horse, you idiot," she laughed, "the accent. I've *never* heard anyone who really speaks that way."

"You never heard my grandfather. So how about it?"

"Sounds great. I haven't had a chance to ride in ages."

Marshall called again Wednesday night, and Thursday.

"Hello?"

"It's me."

"I thought it might be."

"You said I could call."

"I know, but every day?"

"Do you really mind?"

Jessie thought about that a minute. She didn't like aggressive men, didn't like being pressured, but somehow she no longer felt that way about *this* man. Strange.

"No," she admitted.

"Good. What did you do today?"

"Same old thing. How about you?"

"Me too, but I heard a rumor my coyote might be about to do some serious business."

"What will you do now?"

"They haven't decided."

"Oh."

"Jess?"

"Hmmm?"

"I can hardly wait to see you tomorrow."

His husky voice sent a thrill skittering across the back of Jessie's neck and down her arms. She didn't answer.

"Can . . . may I pick you up at your place?"

Jessie hesitated. He'd spoken again in the low, husky tone that turned her insides to warm gelatin.

"Jess?"

"Ye—" she cleared her throat and tried again. "Yes, come over."

She gave him directions, and they hung up. She sat staring at the phone for a long time, wondering if she'd done the right thing.

Marshall arrived twenty minutes early and decided to wait for Jessie on the inviting front porch, where a striped silver cat sat grooming itself. As he reached for the gate latch, a compact bundle of black fur shot around the corner of the house, coming to a stiff-legged stop on the other side of the gate and challenging Marshall with a low, throaty growl.

The thick ruff of fur around the Chow's head stood out like a lion's mane. Small, intelligent eyes glittered from its short-muzzled face as the growl again rolled from its throat.

Marshall slowly withdrew his hand from the

gate, noticing for the first time the BEWARE OF DOG sign. "Well, hello there, big fella," he murmured softly, "aren't you a beauty?"

The cat, startled by the dog's charge, had leapt up on a chair and now also studied Marshall suspiciously. With these two around, Jessie didn't need any big brothers, he thought wryly, then set about making friends.

When Jessie drew up in front of her home, she couldn't believe her eyes. There sat Marshall on her porch, scratching Nan behind his small pointed ears! "What . . . how did . . ."

"Hi, I've got a new buddy," Marshall greeted.

The dog trotted down the short path to meet his mistress. "Some watchdog you are," Jessie grumbled. Picking up on her displeasure, the dog immediately swung back to Marshall, fur bristling. "Nan, no! It's okay," Jessie soothed.

"That's a very responsive dog," Marshall observed as he rose cautiously to his feet.

"Yep." Jessie reached down and rubbed between the dog's ears. "Chow's tend to be very loyal and protective, don't they, Nan?"

"Nan?"

"Short for '*Black Pearl of Nan Hai*.' Nan Hai is the South China Sea." Jessie propped her fists on her hips. "But both you guys are in trouble. How'd you get past the gate? Did you drug my dog?"

Marshall chuckled. "No, nothing so sinister."

"Well?"

He shrugged. "Just a little patience, a little sweet talk, and a little beef jerky."

"Food. I should've known," Jessie snorted in disgust.

Nan dropped his head and looked ashamed.

"I suppose you've met Sheba, too."

Jessie reached the porch and produced her house key. Marshall held the screen open while she unlocked the front door.

"Yeah, but she's been busy ignoring me. Guess the jerky was too spicy for her."

Marshall held the screen door while Jessie, the cat, then the dog all filed into the house. When at last he too stepped inside, he liked what he saw.

He didn't know what he'd expected Jessie's home to look like, but certainly not this. A pair of comfortable-looking wing chairs sat to one side of a fireplace, facing a flowered sofa on the other side. On a small decorative table separating the chairs lay a cut crystal candy dish and a small photograph of a sandy-haired man and a Native American woman in an antique picture frame. The room held an eclectic mixture of furniture styles, but everything fit together nicely, giving it a feeling of welcome and comfort. On a stand in the corner, light reflected off the polished surface of an aged guitar.

"Have a seat," Jessie called from the kitchen, "I'll be with you as soon as I've fed these two."

Marshall lowered himself to the sofa and propped one booted ankle on his knee. "I like your place," he called to her.

"Thanks." Suddenly she stood beside him, a chilled cola in her outstretched hand. "Would you like a bite to eat before we go?"

Marshall took the proffered can from long graceful fingers. "No, thanks, but get yourself something if you want, there's no rush."

"You're sure? It's no trouble, I have all kinds of sandwich fixings."

"I'm sure."

"Okay. Give me a minute to change, then."

Marshall studied his companion surreptitiously as he steered the Jeep away from town. She'd emerged from her bedroom in faded jeans, a plaid shirt, and Western boots, a straw cowboy hat in her hand. The garments were all well worn and looked comfortably at home on her frame.

He returned his attention to the road and found he didn't have to be looking at Jessie to see her. She'd twisted her hair into a coil at the nape of her neck, and the effect was nothing short of elegant. Elegant! In faded jeans and scuffed boots, this tall, willowy woman looked more elegant than all the society belles Marshall could ever remember seeing; her carriage as regal as that of any monarch. She might come off as some kind of ice maiden if it weren't for the temper that lay beneath her poised veneer, he thought. A grin tugged the corner of his lips as he remembered her very human flaw.

They traveled in silence, Marshall lost in thought and Jessie lounging back in her seat, tapping a foot in time to the country song on the radio. When they left the road to turn into the ranch gates, Jessie straightened in her seat. Marshall pulled to a halt by the stables, and Jessie alighted without waiting for him to get her door and ran to throw her arms around the man who'd appeared from the shadowed doorway.

"Jessie! I'll be switched, how are you, girl? Marsh, why didn't you tell me who your lady friend was?"

Jessie kissed the man's cheek, then grinned up into the weathered face as Jim Hawkins held her to his side with an arm around her waist.

"I take it you two know each other?" Marshall asked dryly.

Jim laughed and Jessie continued to grin. "Know her? Shoot fire, when she finished college I lost the best stable hand I've ever had. Tried to talk her into hiring on with me full time, but I guess she wanted to try something more ladylike for a change," the man teased.

"Now, Jim, that's not true and you know it," Jessie argued. "I told you I'd be glad to come back to work for you just as soon as you provided health and retirement benefits. Are you ready to make an offer?"

Everyone laughed, then Jim complained, "Sassy little Injun, ain't she?"

Marshall's gaze cut sharply to Jessie, but she continued to smile at the older man, who patted her hip and said, "Marsh said his lady could ride, but he didn't know how well, so I haltered Chardonnay." Jessie wrinkled her nose at him. "I know, but don't fret, I'll have Usdi ready in a jiffy."

Jessie's eyes lit up. "You still have her?"

The older man hugged her waist, then released her, answering gruffly, "Of course we still have her. She's yours, ain't she?"

Jessie grabbed him and kissed his cheek again. "I love you."

"Yeah, yeah, you say that to all the guys."

"I do not! And I'm perfectly able to saddle a horse by myself, thank you."

Jessie flitted off into the shadows of the stables, leaving the two men staring after her, one in shock and one with a fond smile on his lips.

Jim glanced at Marshall and took pity on him. "Didn't know about me and Jessie, huh?"

Marshall's eyes narrowed as he swung his attention back to his friend. "No," he replied levelly, "can't say as I did."

Jim laughed and clapped the younger man on the shoulder. "Then I guess I'd better fill you in before you take a swing at me," he teased. "My wife is a cousin to Jessie's mother. Jessie worked for me starting in seventh or eighth grade, saving her money for college. She's a real good hand with the horses. By the time she turned sixteen, I had her doing some of the training. She can turn the greenest animal into a proper riding mount fit for the worst tenderfoot."

"She trained Usdi?" Marshall guessed.

"Trained her? She delivered her. I'd probably lost mare and foal both if Jessie hadn't been here to lend a hand. Even though she wouldn't take any credit or payment, I've always told her the filly belongs to her. As you can see, she doesn't really accept that either, except that she named it. And, yes, she handled its training."

Jessie emerged from the double doorway leading a handsome black-and-white paint. The filly's markings immediately conjured up images in Marshall's mind of war ponies with feather-trimmed halters and brightly colored blankets.

Marshall could picture Jessie in a fringed and beaded buckskin dress astride the animal, bare legs gripping its sides, her hair streaming free down her back. His mouth went dry and he swallowed hard.

Unaware of the commotion she was stirring up, Jessie smiled at Marshall. "We're ready, how about you?"

Jim watched the emotions playing over the younger man's face and coughed to cover a laugh. "Ah, we've been shootin' the breeze here, Jessie. Why don't you warm your pony up by riding over to the house and saying hello to Nonnie before you and Marsh ride out?"

"Okay. You'll meet me over there?"

Marshall nodded, unable to get sound past his dry throat.

Jessie swung into the saddle and cantered off. Behind her Jim's laughter filled the air.

"What's so funny?" Marshall managed to snarl.

"You, boy, you. It's a good thing we're as well acquainted as we are, and that I like you, otherwise I might have to take a horsewhip to your hide."

"What the devil are you talking about?"

Jim chuckled and shook his head. "I'm talking about the way you're looking at our girl like she's a rabbit and you're an underfed wolf. When you called to say you wanted to take a lady friend riding, you didn't mention you were in love with the woman."

Marshall sighed. "Is it that obvious?"

"Yup. When did you two meet?"

"You won't believe this."

"Try me."

"A couple of weeks ago. This is our second date."

Jim turned a stunned expression on the younger man. "Criminy!"

"Yeah," Marshall muttered, "criminy."

"Does she feel the same?"

"Hardly. Jess has a distinct distrust of lawmen."

Jim waved a hand negligently. "Not just lawmen, men in general."

"So I've gathered."

"You really love her, or is it just a healthy male reaction?"

"There's that, to be sure, but Jim, I think I'm falling fast. What should I do?"

"Don't hurt her. If you do, I might have to kill you."

"Somehow, I doubt she's the one in danger of being hurt."

"Don't kid yourself, boy. Jessie's all bristle and barbs sometimes, but that's just to cover what's inside. She's the warmest, most loving girl

I've ever known, but she's shy. Never did date much and for some reason she's decided she can't trust men, so she hides in the safety of animals and children."

"I figured as much."

"Yeah, well, she's going to be wondering where we are, and if you don't want to have to tell her what we've been discussing, you'd better get the saddle on that horse of yours. We can continue this later."

Marshall led his horse to the house, walking beside Jim. By the time they reached the porch where Jessie had tied her mount, the two women stood there waiting for them. Marshall had seen Jim's wife only a few times before, but seeing her now, he realized how much she resembled the photograph in Jessie's living room.

Jessie took one look at his horse and started laughing.

Marshall took offense. "Is there a problem?"

"Of course not," Jessie chuckled. "I just can't believe the coincidence. The only other paint on the place belongs to you?"

Marshall relaxed and patted the horse's neck. "Looks that way."

"He's as beautifully marked as Usdi."

"Thank you."

"Since you're both here," Jim put in, "I might as well tell you I've been considering breeding the two. Any offspring of theirs has got to be one fine animal. Think it over and let me know what you decide, okay?"

Marshall and Jessie glanced at each other. They both blushed and quickly dropped their eyes, swinging into their saddles and cantering out of the yard side by side.

Chapter Five

Marshall leaned from his saddle to unlatch the gate. "Want to go out across the pastures?"

"That's fine. How well do you know the landscape here?"

"I ride it almost weekly. Why?"

"Good," Jessie replied as Marshall fastened the gate behind them. A sly grin crossed her face just before she put her heels to the mare's sides. "I'll race you to the pond!"

"Hey! No fair!"

But Marshall didn't lag far behind. Jessie bent low over the paint's neck, urging her on with words of encouragement. The wind tore at her sleek black hair, feathering strands loose from the tight bun. She laughed with the sheer joy riding gave her, the sound floating back to tickle the ear of her pursuer.

Marshall had closed the distance to only half a length when Jessie veered towards a stand of cottonwood trees. He hesitated, then decided to stay to the open field. The way might be a little longer, but his horse's strength in a full run should make up for the mare's ability to finesse her way through the trees. He watched as the females disappeared into the grove. Man, but the woman could ride!

A grin split his rugged face as he urged, "Come on, Scout, we can't let a couple of girls beat us!" The horse fairly flew as they dipped down into a wide creek bed, then scrambled easily up the shallow bank. Marshall caught a flash of white off to his left through the shadows of the trees.

His heart lurched in his chest as he remembered that the creek bed edged the cottonwood grove, but turned deep and narrow at the far end. How long had it been since Jessie had ridden this area? She would reach the small gorge before he could warn her, but Marshall slapped his horse anyway.

Barely within shouting distance when Jessie burst from the woods, Marshall watched time stand still when horse and rider thundered to the edge of the ravine. His heart lodged in his throat, choking off his air as, mane flying, rider bent low over its neck, the pony lifted in slow motion, sailed over the steep drop and landed gracefully on his side of the cut, continuing its headlong flight without a break in stride.

He cursed in relief and admiration, then bent as low as possible in the saddle, urging Scout to greater speed with voice and heels.

Both riders careened to a halt at the same time, several yards apart, their animals' hooves spraying sand into the air at the water's edge.

Jessie was laughing, breathless, her face flushed. "I can't believe it," she gasped, "a tie!"

"Tie my foot," Marshall huffed as he dismounted, his heart still thundering against his breastbone from the fright she'd given him. "You had a head start. If you subtract that, I won."

"Not on your life," Jessie argued as she dropped lightly to the ground.

Marshall reached her, leading his horse, and together they walked the animals to cool them down. "Normally, I'd give a lady a handicap, but not in this case," he insisted.

"Why, because you don't consider me a lady?"

At the odd tone in Jessie's voice, Marshall clapped a large hand on the back of her neck, slipping it under the heavy coil of hair. "Don't be ridiculous! It's because you, lady, ride better than a professional cowboy!"

"Thank you."

"You're welcome. I win."

Jessie smacked his arm and laughed. They rubbed their horses down with handfuls of grass, then loosed them to drink. Jessie dropped to the ground under an oak tree and removed her hat, drawing an arm across her forehead. "I haven't had a workout like that in forever," she sighed, leaning back against the trunk.

Marshall sank to the grass beside her, then stretched out and unceremoniously plopped his head down in her lap.

"Excuse me?"

He grinned up at her before tipping his hat over his face. "I won."

"And you think that misconception gives you privileges?"

"Yep."

Jessie lifted his hat to find him still grinning, eyes sparkling up at her. She swatted the top of his head with the hat, then dropped it back over his face.

Closing her eyes, Jessie rested her head back against the tree, letting her hands trail in the grass at her sides. Overhead, mockingbirds ran through their repertoire and in the distance a dog barked. In a few more weeks frogs and cicadas would add their accompaniment and mosquitoes would fill the air.

"I think we were both surprised today," Jessie commented.

When Marshall didn't answer, she thought he'd fallen asleep. She unconsciously lifted one hand from the grass and laid it on his chest. He instantly covered it with one of his own.

"I've been surprised in more ways than one today," he murmured, "but I suppose you're talking about us both knowing Jim."

"Yes."

"Yeah, that was a surprise all right. For a while there I thought I'd reunited you with a long-lost lover."

Marshall felt Jessie tense beneath him, but then she relaxed and taunted, "Jealous, Abbott?"

He squeezed the hand on his chest and grinned. "Sure am!"

Jessie tried to pull her hand free, but Marshall wouldn't allow it. "You know," he continued lazily from under his hat, "I thought he'd pronounced his own death sentence when he called you a sassy little Indian, but you didn't blink an eye. How come?"

"Because he didn't mean anything by it."

"If I did the same thing, you'd run me over with my own Jeep," he challenged.

"Probably."

Marshall reached up with his free hand, removed his hat from his face, and tossed it aside. "Why, Jess?"

She studied his face for a moment, then shifted her gaze. The question was about more than Jim's teasing and she knew it. Her fingers idly dug small acorns from the grass as she organized her thoughts, seeking a way to explain the wall she'd built around herself. Finally, she sighed.

"When I was little, my father's job caused us to move around quite a bit, from one small town to another. It seemed I was always the new one in class. That in itself can make a child an outsider, but when you factor in my shyness and then my mother being 'a real live Indian,' you magnify that separateness." She gave a small chuckle, sad even to her own ears.

"To make matters even worse, I achieved most of my height by fifth grade. Talk about an ugly duckling! I don't think there was a boy taller than I until halfway through high school."

She fell silent, and Marshall squeezed her hand, encouraging her to continue.

"Jim is family. He loves me like a daughter and I know it. It doesn't matter to him if I'm half Indian or half poodle, five foot ten or five foot nothing. He accepts me for who I am, not what I am."

"And you think I don't?"

Jessie glanced down to find Marshall watching her with somber eyes. She gave a little shrug. "I don't know you that well. All I know is what you say, and that it might be true. With Jim I know it's true. He's proved himself."

"Oh? How?"

Jessie pursed her lips and looked out over the pond. "By marrying Nonnie and treating her with respect. He's one of the most devoted husbands I've ever seen. She's Native American and he loves her."

"So he's proved himself to you by loving an Indian woman?"

"I guess."

Marshall suddenly rolled to a sitting position, cupped the back of Jessie's neck, and brushed his thumb along her jaw in light strokes. His gaze met hers, silently commanding her not to look away this time. Just before their lips met, he whispered, "Then I'm proving myself, too, Jess."

Panicked, Jessie grabbed his wrist in an attempt to break his grip. She didn't want to hear this! He didn't mean it! Her slender hand strained, pulling hard against thick bone and corded muscle to no avail.

Marshall heard her quick intake of breath as he raised his other hand to gently cradle her cheek. Jessie had been protesting, and he was about to end the kiss, but suddenly she clutched his shoulders. Her lips softened, and she acquiesced.

Marshall wrapped his arms around her, pulling Jessie away from the tree to hold her tightly against his chest. The kiss deepened and they lost track of everything else.

Finally, Marshall reluctantly eased up, relaxing his arms, softening the kiss, giving her a chance to withdraw if she wished. Jessie continued to rake his scalp with her nails as she ran her hands through his hair. Then she drew back, ending the kiss. She leaned against the tree again, her breathing labored, eyes closed. After a moment she reached out, captured his hand, and pressed the back of it to her heart, drawing a deep breath.

Marshall leaned over and gently kissed her forehead. He could feel the strong heartbeats pounding her body. Lifting her free hand, he pressed it to his own chest, wanting to share with her the knowledge that his heart raced as wildly as her own.

"We should have stayed on the horses," Jessie murmured.

Matt tenderly brushed a loose strand of hair back from her cheek. "Why? This time you won."

Her eyes flew open and Marshall easily read the distrust reflected in them. He shrugged one shoulder and gave her a lopsided grin before dropping his gaze. "What can I say? You've got a slave for life."

"Right," Jessie snorted, scrambling to her feet. "And tomorrow hell freezes over."

She brushed off the seat of her jeans with two angry swipes and stalked off to retrieve her horse. Marshall sighed, shook his head, then got up to join her.

They rode in silence for nearly an hour, sometimes loping along a dirt road, sometimes walking the horses through forested land thick with undergrowth. At last Marshall had to break the tension.

"Jess, I'm sorry that you're upset with me."

She glanced at him, then away.

"What can I do to make it better?"

"You make it sound like I skinned my knee."

"We skinned more than that, didn't we?"

She didn't answer.

"What did we hurt? Your pride? Your sense of independence? What?"

Jessie sighed. Marshall Abbott had to be the most persistent man she'd ever met. "Nothing is hurt, Mr. Abbott."

"Then why are you so upset?"

Jessie allowed her mare to stop. Marshall reined in Scout and rested folded arms on his saddle horn while he waited for an answer.

"I don't know," she said in exasperation. Marshall grinned and straightened in his saddle, but before he could speak, Jessie added, "But it probably has something to do with the feeling that someone's trying to play me for a fool, and I find that insulting."

"I am not!"

Jessie's eyebrows raised over dark amused eyes. "You aren't what?"

"Insulting you."

"You don't think that 'slave for life' line is insulting to my intelligence?"

"Not when it's true."

"There you go again. You'd better quit while you're ahead, Mr. Abbott."

Marshall reached to touch her, but Jessie thumped her heels into Usdi's sides and raced away. The woman wasn't ready to hear that he thought he loved her.

"Jessie! Where'd you leave Marsh?"

Jessie swung down and grinned at Jim. "I think I lost him when I cut through the oaks and jumped that dead tree."

Jim chuckled and shook his head. "Poor Marsh, I'll bet you led him a merry chase this afternoon." He winked and added, "In more ways than one."

Jessie blushed and busied herself with tending to her horse. She'd no more than removed the saddle when her companion came riding up, muttering under his breath.

"Have a nice ride, Marsh?" Jim asked innocently.

Marshall shot him a malevolent look, and Jim gave a hoot of laughter.

"You kids coming up to the house? Nonnie will likely have dinner on soon."

"Not this time," Jessie answered, "I told her not to expect us. I'll call her tomorrow."

Jim looked at Marshall, but he remained silent, so the older man just nodded his head. "I'll see you later then."

When he'd disappeared around the side of the stables, Jessie glanced at Marshall. "I hope you don't mind. Nonnie wanted us to stay, but she looked awfully tired. If I'd agreed, she would have spent the whole afternoon in the kitchen fixing one of her special meals."

"No, I don't mind." Marshall smiled and added gently, "As long as you share a meal with me."

"You're impossible."

"I try."

Jessie laughed. "Okay, but it'll have to be drive-in hamburgers or something like that. We're both too filthy to go anywhere else."

"Sold."

In companionable silence, they groomed their horses then cleaned their tack before putting both away. Jessie gave her mare a fond pat on its rump. "See you later, girl."

Marshall closed the stall door and latched it. "Have you thought anymore about what Jim suggested? The two of them are practically guaranteed to produce a prize foal."

Jessie turned and assessed the stallion. She couldn't disagree. "What's his name?"

"Scout."

Jessie wrinkled her nose. "Scout?"

"Don't be snide. When I first saw him, his markings reminded me of Tonto's horse. You know, on the Lone Ranger?"

"I know who Tonto is, kemmo sabe," Jessie said dryly.

"Well . . ." Marshall trailed off. "By the way, what does Usdi's name mean?"

"Baby."

"Baby? That's all, just *baby*? And you have the nerve to scoff at the name I gave my horse!"

"It's a perfectly good name," Jessie defended. "And yes, I think she and Scout would be nicely suited."

Jessie then strode off, leaving Marsh a step behind her.

They picked up a bucket of chicken on the way back to Jessie's house. Marshall spoke little, trying to decipher the enigma that was Jessica Holgrave. Inside the beautiful woman with a quick mind and deeply ingrained sense of justice lurked the little girl who was chased across playgrounds in childish games of cowboys and Indians. Games Jessie hadn't wanted to play. He suspected she might also look in the mirror and occasionally still see an ugly duckling. Not possible!

Jessie kept silent as well. Her thoughts were on Marshall. More specifically, on the way he'd kissed her under the oak tree.

Nan charged into the front yard when they pulled up, not yet familiar with Marshall's vehicle, but as soon as he spied his mistress he laid his ears back and wagged his body joyously.

The couple entered the gate and Nan gave Marshall's hand only a cursory sniff before turning his attention back to Jessie and the bucket of chicken.

"He sure goes all-out to greet you."

Jessie laughed. "Not me so much as the food. That dog is ninety-nine percent appetite."

Marshall took the chicken bucket and held it along with the sack containing rolls and side dishes while Jessie dug for her key. Since his arms were full, she held the doors and motioned him into the house ahead of her, taking private satisfaction in knowing it bothered him to precede her.

"Where can I wash up?"

"There's a bathroom in the hall to your left. There should be towels and washcloths on the racks."

Jessie went to her own bathroom to clean up. She stripped off her shirt and bra and gave herself a quick scrubbing. Donning a clean bra and fresh shirt, she ran the brush through her hair and tied it back with a scarf. She started out of the room, then glanced in the mirror. A quick application of eyeliner and a dab of lipstick later, she rejoined Marshall in the kitchen.

He looked as if he'd also stripped to the waist to clean up. His hair was wet and his face shiny, his hands and forearms scrubbed clean. Jessie realized she was staring at him and quickly moved to cover her discomfort.

"Ah, we, ah, can eat in here or in the living room. Or out on the porch."

"Here is fine. What can I do to help?"

"Fill the glasses. I have tea, soda, or milk. Ice is in the freezer."

Jessie watched from the corner of her eye as he filled one large glass with milk, then turned to her. "What do you want?"

"Milk, please."

"We have a lot in common."

"How do you figure that?"

"Well, we both like milk, paint horses, Jim and Nonnie, Mike and Ellen, fried chicken, assorted animals, and challenges."

"I don't like challenges."

Marshall leaned his hips against the counter and crossed his arms over his chest. "Yes, you do, you just won't admit it."

Jessie ignored him as she got down plates and set them on the kitchen table. He was blocking the silverware drawer, however, so she had to ask him to move. He took one step to the side and no more, making her come nearer to get the needed tableware.

Jessie felt the heat climbing her cheeks. Marshall was so close she could smell the soapy fragrance on his skin. She knew he goaded her purposely, but couldn't help her reaction.

Turning from him, she dropped a fork, and had to return to the drawer for another. Annoyed with his effect on her, she slammed the drawer shut this time. He just grinned.

Nan sat by the table, begging as usual, providing Jessie with a welcome topic of conversation when Marshall asked about him. While they ate, Jessie extolled the merits and the foibles of the breed in general, and of Nan in particular. Marshall then related stories of the dogs he'd had while growing up, after which Jessie asked, "You don't have one now?"

"No, not with living in a condo and coming and going like I do. Sometimes I'm not home for several days in a row."

"Oh?"

Marshall nodded as he chewed half a dinner roll, having given the other half to Nan. He swallowed and explained, "Like week after next, for instance. I'm leaving for the valley early Monday and who knows when I'll be back."

Leaving? Although only half an hour ago Jessie had wished he'd do that very thing, she now felt bereft at the thought, and slightly panicked that he'd be so far away. "The valley?"

"Yes, the valley. My investigation, remember? The coyote?" he reminded her. "I have to go look for him."

Jessie rose quickly and carried her plate to the sink in an excuse to turn her back on him. She didn't want Marshall to see how upset she'd become, especially when she didn't understand why herself. She'd almost forgotten he was a law officer, though she still struggled to reject him as an aggressive male. And even her reasons for that were becoming muddied. Beside her, Marshall turned on the tap and rinsed his plate. Jessie jumped and skittered sideways; she hadn't heard his approach.

"Could we sit out on the porch awhile?"

Jessie nodded and wordlessly led the way.

Why did she feel so let down, so abandoned? She barely knew the man, for Pete's sake.

She sat down in the middle of her porch swing, her mind on Marshall's imminent departure. A moment later, she glanced up to see him standing nearby, studying her. She raised a brow in question and he gestured to a spot next to her on the swing.

"May I?"

"Oh! Yes, of course, I'm sorry."

She scooted to one end and Marshall sat down near the center, reaching for her and placing an arm behind her shoulders. "Not so far, scoot back or the swing will go crooked," he said, easily sliding her back to his side.

Then he braced his feet and set the swing in motion. "That's better." His arm around Jessie's shoulders, Marshall drew a deep breath then released it slowly, savoring the evening air.

"Now this is the life. A good day's exercise, a full stomach, a porch swing, a dog, and. . ." he paused as he pulled Jessie closer, dropping his arm behind her back to her waist and positioning her head on his shoulder with his free hand, "a beautiful woman."

Jessie tried to pull away, but he'd anticipated her reaction and held her in place. She lifted her face to rail at him, and he caught her jaw in his hand. With no more warning than that, Marshall

lowered his mouth to hers and sent Jessie spiral-
ing off into space. Long before he lifted his head,
she'd grabbed a handful of shirt as though hanging on for dear life.

"Jess," he whispered, "Jess."

His thumb rubbed back and forth over her
lower lip, the calloused skin sending a prickling
sensation down Jessie's arms. She fought the urge
to capture it with her teeth, to taste it with her
tongue. Marshall sighed and tucked her head into
the hollow of his shoulder. Jessie snuggled down
comfortably and wrapped her arm around his
middle. They sat that way for quite a while, the
chains on the swing squeaking as Marshall
pushed them in a slow lulling rhythm.

The air cooled as full dark descended and Jessie shivered. Marshall squeezed her once, then
released her and stretched to his feet. "I'd better
be going now."

He held out a hand and pulled her up beside
him, then stroked her cheek with his knuckles.
"I've had the most fantastic day," he murmured.
"Being with you is . . . is, just incredible. Thank
you, Jess."

Jessie dropped her gaze to his boot tips as a
blush warmed her face. "Thank you. I enjoyed it
too."

He tipped her face up for a parting kiss, then
grumbled, "I don't want to go, you know."

Jessie gave him a quick little smile in response. He brushed her face with his fingertips. "Good night, sweetheart."

Marshall turned and bounded down the steps and out the gate, as if being near her one more second would be more than he could bear. Just before slamming the door on his Jeep, he called back, "I'll see you tomorrow."

Tomorrow? You mean I'll have to go through all of this again tomorrow?

Chapter Six

Jessie rose early, pushed aside thoughts of Marshall's promised visit, and began her household chores. She had entirely too much to do to waste any more time with that overgrown . . . that overgrown . . . anyway, she had too much to do!

Jessie changed her bed and bath linens and started her laundry. She ran the vacuum cleaner and scoured her bathroom. When she went to tidy the hall bath, she found the cloth and towel Marshall used the previous evening. Hesitantly, she picked them up and found they were still damp. Damp from washing and drying his body.

Spinning from the room, she hurried to throw the two items into the washing machine with the rest of the towels, then grabbed up a bucket and brush and hurried outside. If he called, she wouldn't be there to answer.

Jessie turned on the hose and called Nan. The dog loved to play in the water. He'd leap and snap at the stream from the hose and run through the sprinkler. He didn't much care for being washed, but since it meant getting to play, he tolerated it. Jessie soaped him down, then scrubbed him gently with the brush, working the lather down to his skin. She held him by his mane as she rinsed him off, then she let him cavort in the spray. He stopped and shook himself, completing the job of drenching Jessie, then barreled through the water again, running in tight circles.

"Is this a private game, or can anyone play?"

Jessie's head snapped around. Nan gave a friendly bark then ran to the gate to greet Marshall.

"I . . . I guess I didn't hear the phone out here."

Jessie looked adorable in her disheveled state, and Marshall smiled. "I didn't call. If you'll remember, I told you last night I'd see you today. Weren't you expecting me?"

"Not really," Jessie lied.

"Well, now that I'm here, do you need any help?"

"No, we're finished. This is his reward for standing still for a bath."

"I can hold the hose while you go dry off," Marshall offered.

"Thanks, but I still have things to do."

"Such as?"

Jessie sighed. The word *persistent* sprang to mind again, but she believed it an understatement in regard to Marshall Abbott. "I've laundry to finish, a kitchen floor to mop, grocery shopping to do . . ."

Marshall stood with his hands on his hips, eyeing her suspiciously. "Sounds like a lot for just one day. I don't believe you usually do *all* your domestic chores on Saturday. I think you're trying to run me off, and it isn't going to work."

"You're welcome to sit and watch if you'd like," Jessie offered sweetly.

"As much pleasure as that would give me, I have a better idea. If I help, you'll be finished earlier and can spend some time with me. I'll do the floor while you finish what needs doing in the house. We can go to the grocery store together."

"But . . ."

Marsh held up his hand for silence. "Where's the mop?"

Jessie folded laundry and reloaded the washing machine while Marshall mopped the floor. She watched him out of the corner of her eye and was surprised to see he knew exactly what to do. After rinsing the floor, he asked where she kept the wax.

"I only wax it once a month or so," she admitted, "and I did that last week."

"Okay, are you ready to go to the store?"

"I suppose."

Marshall lifted an eyebrow. "You don't sound as gung ho as you did earlier."

"I, ah, only need a couple of things."

"I see."

Jessie peeked up at him, expecting a scowl, but instead finding a self-satisfied smile. She frowned.

"Come on, Jess," he teased, "don't be a sore loser. Tell me what you need and I'll get it while you finish your wash."

She shook her head in exasperation and sighed. "Okay, get a half gallon of milk, a loaf of bread, and a dozen eggs, please."

Jessie went to her purse for money, but Marshall brushed it aside. "We can settle up when I get back. Are you sure that's all? No food for the furries?"

"No, that's all. Thanks."

He grinned and plopped a kiss on her forehead. "My pleasure."

When his Jeep pulled away from the house, Jessie slumped to the sofa. What on earth was she going to do with the man? He'd just entered her life and blithely taken over, or at least tried to. A reluctant smile lifted her lips at the picture of him bent over her spindly mop, attacking her kitchen floor with gusto. She wondered what the other Rangers in his barracks would say if they knew about it.

By the time Marshall returned, she'd put away the folded laundry, brushed her hair and pinned it up in a coil, put on a touch of makeup, and changed into a clean shirt.

He tapped on the screen door with the toe of his boot, his arms laden with grocery bags. "Looks to me like you improvised on my shopping list," Jessie observed as she held the door open.

"Just a little. I got hot dogs to cook in the backyard, and chips and relish to go with them, and I got some ice cream for dessert."

"I invited you for dinner?"

"No, I'm inviting you. I'll even do the cooking."

Jessie laughed in spite of herself. Marshall's enthusiasm and self-assurance swept over her wariness like a storm surge. She just couldn't stand against it.

"You're a gourmet chef, I can tell," she teased.

He grinned. "I get by."

Under her breath, Jessie muttered, "I'll just bet you do."

"So what's next? Wash the windows? Clean the oven? Roof the garage?"

Jessie shot him the go-to-blazes look he remembered from last week and answered, "That's it until the load in the dryer is finished."

"Good. Come sit down with me so we can continue getting to know each other."

Marshall tugged on her hand until she followed him to the couch. He sat, pulling her with him and wrapping an arm around her.

"Marshall," she warned.

He ignored her and pointed to the photograph on the small table. "Is that your grandparents?"

"No, my parents."

"Oh? You must be the youngest, then."

"Yes, Mom was almost forty when she had me."

"You come from a large family?"

"I suppose. Mother had eight children, but two died shortly after birth. Her second and fifth, I think."

"So you grew up with five sisters?"

"No, I grew up with four brothers and one sister."

"You told me you didn't have any older brothers."

"When?"

"At the hospital, when we were sitting in the waiting room."

Jessie shot him a sly grin. "I believe you asked if I had any older brothers or brothers at all who were bigger than you, and I don't. My brothers are five feet, eleven inches to six foot one. Sammy might be six foot two by now, but you outweigh him, so even if you weren't taller, that still makes you bigger. Jaquin, Manny, and Pete are all built like fighting bulls, but are shorter than you."

"In other words, with the possible—and note I said *possible*—exception of Sammy, your brothers could likely wipe the floor with me."

"Yep," Jessie admitted cheerfully.

Marshall scowled at the grinning woman he held in the crook of his arm. "I do believe, Jessica Holgrave, that you are a hard woman after all."

The grin died and Jessie peered up at him, all wide-eyed innocence. "Why? Were you planning something that might upset my brothers? A fine upstanding lawman like yourself? I can't believe it."

Marshall threw back his head and laughed. He laughed so hard that Nan set up a fuss at the screen, barking and jumping.

"Nan, quiet!" Jessie ordered. Out on the porch, the dog dropped to his belly obediently, and Jessie looked at Marshall. "You, too."

A mischievous glint in his eye, he replied,

"Whatever the lady wants," then wrapped her in his arms and proceeded to kiss her senseless.

When the dryer buzzer went off, Jessie had no idea what the sound meant or where it was coming from. Finally, Marshall raised his head and murmured, "How do you shut that racket off?"

"What racket?"

He continued nuzzling her ear. "That buzzer."

"Buzzer?"

His lips slid to her throat. "Um-hmm," he said against her skin.

"Oh! The buzzer! The dryer."

Jessie wiggled free and rose unsteadily to her feet. Marshall clung to her hand for a moment and ordered in a husky voice, "Hurry back."

As she tottered away, the thought occurred to Jessie that the man was absolutely lethal!

Head back and eyes closed, Marsh heard only the softest swish of sound before a cold splat of water hit him square on the forehead. His eyes flew open and he sat bolt upright. Jessie stood over him with a cold can of soda.

"Thought you could use some cooling off."

He cocked a brow and reached for her. "I don't want to cool off."

Jessie stepped back quickly, out of his reach. "Sorry about that, but it's next on the agenda."

Marshall sighed and didn't say anything.

"I think I'll wash my car before dinner. If you'd like, we can do your Jeep, too."

Marshall shot her a look that told Jessie washing cars was definitely *not* what he'd like to be doing, but he got to his feet. "Okay, let's go."

On the porch, Marshall took off his boots and socks and rolled his jeans up a couple of turns, then stripped off his shirt. Jessie came out the screen door carrying a bucket.

Soapy water sloshed over the edge of the bucket and soaked her tennis shoes when Jessie stopped dead in her tracks. There, on her porch, was the widest, most beautiful male back Jessie had ever seen. Broad shoulders tapered to a narrow waist; row upon row of knobby muscles flanked the valley of his spine; hard, rounded shoulders topped thickly corded arms.

She'd never guessed he'd look like this. He could undoubtedly take on any one of her brothers. Maybe even all of them at once! Marshall turned his head to glance back over his shoulder, causing the beautiful contours to dance.

"Here, give me that."

He pushed away from the post and reached for the bucket handle. The front of him was no less magnificent than the back. A furious blush climbed Jessie's neck, igniting her cheeks.

"I didn't mean to embarrass you," Marshall

muttered, setting down the bucket and reaching for his shirt.

"What? Oh. Oh, no . . . that is, I mean, that's okay. You'll just get it wet if you put it back on."

He straightened, and Jessie watched all that beautiful muscle shift and glide. "Are you sure you don't mind?" he asked.

"Of course not."

Mind? What mind? Hers was gone, totally blown. If she still had one, she'd insist he cover up immediately, preferably with a horse blanket!

Jessie closed her bedroom door and peeled off her wet jeans, then decided to take a quick shower. In the backyard, Marshall worked at getting charcoal started for the hot dogs, then he would come in and wash up. If she didn't dawdle she'd be out and dressed by the time he finished.

As it happened, she'd been on the patio for several minutes, combing out her tangled hair, when Marshall stepped out in fresh clothes, his hair wet, a gym bag in his hand.

"Hope you don't mind, I used the shower." He lifted the bag in explanation. "I'll be right back."

Jessie heard a car door shut, then he came trotting back around the side of the house.

"You come prepared."

Marsh didn't miss her wary tone. "In my profession I never know where I'll be or when, so I always carry a change with me." He grinned disarmingly. "A good thing, too. Dating you is hard work."

Jessie laughed, then winced when the comb caught on a snag in her hair.

"Let me give you a hand there," Marshall offered, taking the comb from her. "The charcoal needs to burn down some yet."

Jessie started to resist, even though this was her fantasy come true, in fact, *because* this was her fantasy come true. But in the end, she allowed herself the indulgence.

Marshall worked the knot free and pulled the comb to the ends of her hair. Then he started at her hairline, pulling the comb slowly across her scalp and down the back of her neck. When she didn't feel the plastic teeth on her back, Jessie looked over her shoulder to find Marshall perched on the picnic table instead of on the bench. To unsnarl her hair, he had draped it over his thigh. Soon no tangles remained, and the comb made slow nonstop sweeps from hairline to hair ends. It felt absolutely delicious. Jessie drifted for some time in the sensation, then sighed.

"Do you mind me doing this?"

She chuckled. "Are you kidding? I'm only wondering if I can afford your fee."

Marshall sifted the drying hair through his fingers, fanning it across his leg, over her shoulders, just letting it fall where it would. "I couldn't charge you for something I enjoyed so much," he answered, only half teasing. Then he tipped her face up and kissed her forehead. "Time for supper."

Jessie set the table while the franks grilled, using a citronella candle for their centerpiece to discourage the few mosquitoes who'd come out with the lowering sun.

They nearly collided in the kitchen when he came in to warm the buns in the microwave and she was heading out with an armload of condiments. He kissed the end of her nose, grinned, and went on. His casual caress paired with the domesticity of the scene gave Jessie a warm, fuzzy glow. *I could get to like this*, she thought.

Marshall whistled an off-key tune as he removed the plate from the microwave. He and Jessie were making progress. Her thorny disposition was more a matter of occasional prickliness now, and he had a very good feeling about where they were headed. He breathed the sigh of a contented man.

His serenity was short lived. A horrendous riot of noise suddenly erupted from the yard. A sharp bark preceded a furious hiss, a pained howl, and Jessie yelling, "Scat! Shoo, get out of here! Stop that!"

Marshall charged out the door, ready to do battle. "What the heck?"

Jessie clapped her hands together, chasing her pets to the far side of the yard, then sat down and called Nan back to her. She cradled his big head in her lap as she examined his nose, then patted him. "You'll be fine. Now get out of here and behave yourself."

Marshall stood over her, hands on his hips. "What on earth happened?"

"While the hot dogs were unguarded, Sheba helped herself. Nan thought she should share, but she disagreed."

Marshall started laughing. "Is that all? It sounded like World War Three." He reached for the plate of meat and called, "Here, Nan."

"Oh, no, you don't, he's just been reprimanded. You can give him one when we're finished."

"Yes, ma'am," Marshall teased and returned to the kitchen for the buns.

Marshall dried the last dish, put it away, and folded the dishtowel. He leaned his hips against the sink and watched Jessie finish wiping down the countertops. She glanced up, giving him a shy smile, then turned to wipe a ketchup thumbprint off the refrigerator door.

"All done," she chirped brightly when she turned back to him, but he heard the tension in her voice. He wasn't sure what it meant, but he heard it. He dropped an arm around her shoulders. "Walk me to the car?"

He felt her relax. Maybe she'd expected a wrestling match on the couch.

She put an arm around his waist. "Sure."

Standing beside his Jeep, they both started to talk at once.

"Thanks—"

"Jess—"

They chuckled nervously. "Go ahead," Jessie offered.

"No, ladies first."

"I just wanted to thank you for dinner and for helping with the chores."

"I wanted to thank you for letting me."

"You did not."

He laughed, slipping his hands beneath her fall of hair and locking them behind her neck. "You're right. What I really want to thank you for is letting me spend the day with you, even if it was in household drudgery."

He pulled her closer and rested his chin on the top of her head. Jessie's hands settled on his hip bones, as though trying to span his waist. "Ah, Jess," he sighed, "what now?"

She didn't answer. He didn't expect her to. Just

like last night, he didn't want to leave. He didn't ever want to leave again. With a sound that was half sigh, half moan, he closed her in an embrace, pulling her tightly to him. Her arms slid around his waist and she hugged him too, her face pressed into his neck. Marshall couldn't say how long they held each other that way, but it had to substitute for kissing her good night. Feeling as he did, he knew that if he kissed her now, he wouldn't stop until he'd made love to her.

Finally, he slowly released her and asked, "To-morrow?"

She nodded, and before he lost his determination, Marshall kissed her quickly on the forehead and closed himself in the relative safety of his Jeep.

Jessie slid into bed and turned off the lamp on her night table. She smoothed the lightweight blanket and settled comfortably on her pillow. It would be awhile before she fell asleep, though. Too much was going on in her head.

The click of Nan's nails sounded on the kitchen linoleum, then Jessie heard his soft grunt as he dropped to the floor beside her bed for the night. In another minute she felt the mattress give a little by her hip when Sheba jumped up beside her. She reached out a hand in the dark to stroke the cat, who then climbed onto Jessie's stomach, walked the length of her legs, stepped off at her ankles, and curled up at her feet.

She had stood by her front gate for several minutes after Marshall drove off, listening to the sound of his engine until she could no longer distinguish it. When she turned back to the house, it seemed suddenly empty. She'd climbed the porch steps and couldn't help noticing how forlorn an unoccupied swing could look. The living room was too quiet, the kitchen too uncluttered. She wandered from room to room, closing windows, locking up for the night, and it felt as though the life had gone out of her home. Now she lay on her back in the dark, in the wide bed she shared with her cat, and wondered about it.

The day she'd just spent had been filled with only the most ordinary pursuits, yet she couldn't remember one she'd enjoyed more, not even yesterday.

Yesterday had been exhilarating, racing across open meadows, threading through the trees, but she'd been tense, guarded. Today she'd felt more relaxed, less wary than usual. The sobering truth dawned on Jessie. She'd begun to trust Marshall. Not completely, but the seed was sown.

In the dark, Jessie's lips curved into a smile as she thought about his name. Marshall. Marsh Abbott. Marsh bent over the mop. Marsh carrying groceries in the front door. Marsh's kiss on the living room sofa. Marsh combing her hair. A warmth settled in her heart. She hugged herself in the darkened room, overcome by the mellow glow and the feeling that he could be the one. Marshall Abbott could just possibly be the one to sweep her off her feet. The thought scared her to death but didn't dim her smile.

Chapter Seven

Jessie put her purse away and turned to the mirror to remove her earrings, but the doorbell interrupted her. Her heart skipped joyfully and a nervous tremor ran through her body as she hurried to the front door.

"Hello."

Jessie swallowed at the lump in her throat. Lord help her, but he looked wonderful leaning on her door frame like that, with tousled hair, sleepy eyes, and a shy smile. "He—hello," she stammered.

"Am I too early?"

His voice was low and grating this early in the morning, sending Jessie's heart into double time.

"No, no." She held the screen open. "Come in. I . . . I didn't know when you were coming, so I went to early services. I just got back."

"You look very nice."

"Thank you."

Their relationship had reached a new plane yesterday, but this morning it seemed as though they were starting over. Or could it be they were both shying away from what they knew lay ahead?

This is ridiculous, Jessie scolded herself, struggling for calm. *Just act natural. I am,* she thought, *I'm a natural nervous wreck.* "Would you like some coffee?" she offered.

"Yes, as a matter of fact, I would. But there's something else I want first."

Marshall's voice more closely resembled a growl and his eyes were fixed on her mouth. The breath caught in her throat and her lips parted slightly with the quivering sensation that swept through her. She didn't say a word, but her eyes questioned and Marshall answered by pulling her into his arms for a kiss of greeting. He kept it short and light, but it stirred Jessie to her toes.

"Good morning," he whispered against her hair as he pressed her to his chest.

"Good morning."

With a finger under her chin, he tipped her face

up and kissed the tip of her nose. "Now, about that coffee?"

"What's on the agenda for today, painting the house?"

Jessie loved the way Marshall's eyes sparkled when he teased.

"Sounds like a plan. Are you any good at it?" She paused to lick custard from a cream puff off her fingers. "You could start in here, the cabinet doors need it badly."

Marshall laughed and plunged a hand into the sack of pastries he'd brought, coming up with a chocolate eclair. Forsaking the use of silverware, he bit into the confection, leaving a chocolate mustache, and winning a chuckle from Jess.

"Some people's children never grow up," she chided as she dabbed his face with a paper napkin.

In a sudden shift of mood, Marshall caught her hand. He pressed her knuckles to his lips, closed his eyes, and sighed. He lowered their hands to the tabletop and studied them. Then he said quietly, "Jess, I love you."

Jessie tried to snatch her hand away, but Marshall held it firmly, and raised a troubled gaze to hers. "I know it's too soon to tell you," he hurried on, "you hardly know me, but I have to leave soon and I wanted you to know."

He dropped his gaze again and added softly, "I needed for you to know, Jess."

She didn't answer, but Marsh could feel the hand he grasped trembling—or was it his own? The possibility that something could go wrong hung unspoken, yet recognized, between them. The possibility that he could die on some lonely stretch of road and never see her again. Several moments of silence passed before he finally garnered the nerve to look at Jess again. To his surprise, she looked . . . well, calm. Serene might even be a better word. She looked to be at peace. A blush climbed her cheeks and her lashes lowered to avoid his eyes.

"Would you like some more coffee?" she asked quietly.

"Yes, please."

Jessie stood and picked up their cups. When she'd turned her back on him, she allowed herself a deep, cleansing breath. She struggled to maintain an outward calm, but inside a riot was in full progress. Her heart zinged off her ribs, bouncing around like a rubber ball; every nerve ending she possessed quivered and jumped, joyful laughter threatened to bubble over and escape.

Marshall had said he loved her. And in the few minutes of silence while he'd studied their joined hands on the table, Jessie had decided she'd let him.

As for her own feelings, she intended to take it a little slower, but she opened herself to the possibility that he meant what he said. Hadn't he once told her he'd never lie to her? Not quite ready to throw herself heedlessly into this relationship, she admitted in her heart to a growing fondness—and a raging desire—for the tall man with the boyish smile.

Jessie's hands shook when she poured the coffee, but she tried to appear composed as she moved across the room to rejoin him at the table. "So," she began, flashing him a beautiful smile as though he'd never bared his soul to her, "do you really want to paint, or can we go for a drive instead?"

Once again Marshall followed her lead. If she wanted to go for a drive, they'd go for a drive, but he'd much rather explore things of a more personal nature. He sighed and waved his hand toward the front door. "The Jeep's all opened up. If you're wanting wind in your hair, let's go."

"Where to?"

"Wherever you'd like."

"All the way to Brenham? This weekend is the Spring Fling."

"All the way to Brenham for the Spring Fling," he agreed, "whatever that is."

Jessie laughed in a light, joyful burst of sound. "I'll change and be back before your coffee's cooled."

Marshall watched her swing from the room with a tightening sensation in his chest. He'd been in love before, and would in fact be married now, if the girl hadn't backed out after he'd made it plain he intended to remain in law enforcement. But that had been nothing compared to what he was experiencing now. His feelings for Jess were growing at an astounding rate. Morosely, he lifted his cup to his lips, and burned his tongue. Only the first of many pains yet to come, he thought grimly.

The Jeep sped northwest on Highway 290, carrying them to a day of carefree relaxation. Marshall hummed along with the song on the radio, tapping his thumbs on the steering wheel to the beat of the music. Jessie slouched down in her seat, one knee braced against the dashboard, her hair whipping wildly in the wind. She looked over at Marshall and grinned. He smiled and dropped his right hand from the wheel to lace his fingers with hers. Jessie looked away, pointing with her other hand at a large patch of bluebonnets just off the roadway, but didn't take her hand from his.

The air smelled sweet with new growth. Indian paintbrush made vivid red splashes on the roadside and in fields. In some places it mixed with the brilliant bluebonnets in a nature lover's bouquet. Scissor-tailed flycatchers sat on fence wire and turkey vultures wheeled high overhead, riding the thermals.

Marshall looked over at Jess and felt his chest tighten another notch. Skinny jeans, sleeveless chambray shirt, dangling turquoise earrings, sandals, a smile that would melt stone and a body that just wouldn't quit. Marshall didn't believe she looked like anyone's idea of a librarian.

She arched a brow at him. "What's that sneaky little grin for?"

He squeezed her hand. "Nothing."

"You told me you wouldn't lie."

"I was just thinking that you don't look much like any librarian I ever remember seeing before."

Jessie wrinkled her nose at him. "School's out today. I can look like a regular person. I don't have to look like a librarian."

Marshall thought that *regular* didn't exactly describe her either.

In Brenham, Jessie guided him to the old downtown area where the streets were blocked off for the festival. They parked on a side street and he waited while Jess ran a brush through her hair before coiling it up off her neck. Hand in hand, they walked up the street to the area of booths, shops, and music. The streets around the library square were lined with vendors' booths selling crafts, food, and assorted trinkets. On the library steps, a marimba band, made up of high school students, filled the air with the mellow sounds of "Tiny Bubbles."

They paused at one booth and Jessie bought a stained-glass suncatcher in the shape of an intricate starburst to give her mother for Mother's Day. Their next stop was for sausages on sticks and lemonade. Marshall stopped and bought a sterling silver hair buckle, which he presented to Jessie.

She twisted her hair and held it in place with the silver piece, sliding the wooden pick through her hair to hold it. "I thought you liked my hair down."

Marshall laid a hand on the back of her neck and leaned close to her ear. "I do. But I also enjoy being the one to let it down."

In spite of the warm spring air, a shiver prickled down Jessie's back and up her scalp. She cleared her throat. "Do you like old cars?"

"I guess. Why?"

"There's usually an antique car club from Houston that comes to display their cars down that way if you'd like to go look at them."

"Let's see what they brought."

Hand in hand, they walked the two blocks in silence. So much feeling, but each unable or unwilling to put it in words.

For the next hour or so they admired the collection of antique and classic cars and listened to the owners talking about their machines. Jessie fell in love with a 1937 Packard convertible, while Marshall gazed longingly at a 1953 Jaguar XD-120. There were two wide, low Hudsons, one a 1950 Pacemaker and the other a 1954 Hornet, both looking like they'd mean business on a highway. There were 1957 Chevrolets, 1955 Ford Thunderbirds, Model A Fords, Mustangs, and even a 1931 Studebaker which looked brand-new. Jessie regretted not bringing her camera.

Back at the square, Marshall bought a wind chime for Jessie's yard, saying only, "I like wind chimes."

Jessie stopped at a display of earrings and bought a pair for her mother. Marshall started to buy some for her, but she stopped him with a teasing, "Enough already."

They ambled around the rest of the square, their arms around each other's waists. Marshall left her on a bench under an oak tree and came back with funnel cakes. The powdered sugar coated her fingers and Jessie rubbed at it with a napkin before giving up and raising her fingers to lick them. Marshall caught her wrist, murmured "Allow me," and laved them one by one.

Jessie's cheeks warmed with embarrassment . . . and something else. She suddenly wished they were far from this place and completely alone. Marshall's assault on her defenses grew more successful with each passing hour in his company, she realized.

But next week he'd be gone. Jessie could barely stand to think it, let alone say it aloud. She pulled her hand from him and jumped to her feet. "Wait here, I'll be right back."

"What . . . where . . . ?"

"Please?" Her expression fervent, she pleaded, "I'll be right back."

Marshall nodded and watched her hurry away as though on a mission of great importance. To Jessie, it was. She returned shortly with a small packet of tissue paper folded in her hand. Resuming her seat next to him, she hesitantly offered the packet. "When you leave . . . when you go on your assignment, would . . . would you wear this for me?"

Marshall unfolded the paper to reveal a silver cross. It was set with mother of pearl and threaded on a chain of sturdy silver links. Gingerly, he ran one large fingertip down the length of the cross, and swallowed at the lump in his throat. "It's beautiful, Jess, thank you."

Jessie sat motionless, waiting for him to say he'd wear it.

Marshall extended it toward her. "Put it on for me?"

Jessie held it against her lips for a moment, then fastened the chain around his neck. She touched the cross with her fingertips. "My prayers go with it," she murmured.

Marshall took her hand and kissed the backs of her fingers. "I know."

In silent accord, they stood and walked back to the Jeep, their steps slow and measured in the waning afternoon. Marshall opened the door for Jessie, then stopped her for a soft, lingering kiss, after which he cradled her face in his hands and looked deep into her eyes.

Jessie rested her hands against his chest and took advantage of this moment to drink her fill. She studied the curve of his brows, the brown flecks in his eyes, the shape of his nose. Had it once been broken? Probably. The squint lines in the corners of his eyes, the shadow of beard beneath his skin, his sharply etched lips. He had such beautiful lips. Jessie's mouth watered and she directed her attention back to his eyes, soft and loving in the afternoon light, fringed with thick short lashes. She had to reassess her position of this morning. Caution or no, she'd fallen in love with Marshall Abbott, a very Caucasian Texas Ranger.

Marshall saw a flicker of surprise widen the brown eyes he was busy adoring, then saw them soften with an infinite tenderness. He released Jessie's face and reached behind her head to free her hair. When he'd handed her the two parts of the silver buckle, he ran his fingers through the ebony fall, fanning it about her shoulders. He smoothed it, arranged it, petted it, gloried in its heavy satin texture until he was in danger of losing his self-control, then took Jessie's elbow and urged her into the car. "Let's go home," he murmured.

On the return trip, Marshall's hand cupped the back of Jessie's neck under her hair, his thumb and fingers lightly caressing her skin. Jessie's left hand rested on his thigh, absently tracing a pattern on his jeans with a fingernail.

They reached her house and he followed her in the gate. Marshall took her key and unlocked the door. In the kitchen, he reached for the dog food and ordered gently, "Go take your shower so I can comb out your hair for you."

She stopped abruptly and her startled gaze lifted to his.

He brushed the backs of his fingers down her cheek in a feather-light caress and murmured, "I want that memory to take with me."

She nodded silently and turned to do as he asked.

Jessie stood under the running water, concentrating on the feel of it, trying to block from her mind Marshall's imminent departure. She didn't want to think of him in danger.

With her back to the pulsing spray, she lifted her face, letting the fingers of water massage her scalp before sheeting down and off her hair, veiling her in a watery cloak. She could feel each rivulet that streamed down her back, each trickle that snaked over her skin. She reached for the shampoo and lathered the heavy mass until it squeaked.

Pushing back the shower curtain, she stepped from the tub and wrapped her hair in a towel, reached for another, and patted her skin dry. Automatically, she fluffed on powder, rubbed on lotion, and brushed her teeth, just as she did every night before going to bed. Only she wasn't going to bed. Marshall was waiting for her. She pulled on a faded pair of cutoffs and an old T-shirt, then went in search of her comb.

He sat on the living room sofa, a footstool positioned between his legs. He'd put on a fresh shirt and the silver cross glinted at his throat. When he spotted her in the doorway, he patted the stool then held out his hand for the comb. "May I?"

Jessie surrendered—the comb and her heart.

She perched in front of him and Marshall began to work the comb through the ends of her hair. Having done this just last night, he quickly figured out the best way to free the tangles and soon stood to pull the comb through the entire length of her ebony tresses. Jessie closed her eyes when he threaded the teeth in at her hairline then began to gently pull it back, back, over her skull, down her neck, down her shoulders, down her spine.

Marshall repeated the process several times, then set the comb aside. He chafed her upper arms, which had blossomed with goose bumps, then bent to kiss the side of her neck. He lightly nipped the tendon running from her neck and whispered her name before cupping her shoulders and pulling her back against him. "Will you listen now, Jess? Can I tell you now that I love you?"

His breath warmed her neck where he'd buried his face against her skin. He slid his arms around her, pulling her back against his hard chest, and she bent to kiss the muscled arm that pressed her to him. Suddenly she was canted sideways into the crook of his arm as his impatient mouth took hers. Jessie struggled to turn more fully into his embrace so she could hold him, run her hands over his face and shoulders, plunge her fingers in his hair.

He broke the kiss and pressed his forehead to hers. "I love you Jess, you know that, don't you?"

Leaning on the edge of the screen door, Jessie watched him drive away, wondering if she hadn't made the biggest mistake of her life. Marshall had kissed her tenderly, avowed his love, and with each touch, each word, she became more certain that she couldn't live without him. She'd fallen in love with a lawman. She was his: heart, body, and soul. In a few hours he would be gone to God only knew where for God only knew how long. And, only God knew if he would come back. Her chest felt as if someone were twisting a giant corkscrew into it.

When she could no longer hear the sounds of his Jeep moving down the road, she turned back into the house.

Chapter Eight

Only a month of school left. Soon all the library books would be called in and Jessie would need to compile a list of missing books and which students had last checked them out. But not yet.

She wandered around the corner of her desk, skimming her fingertips over its polished surface, thinking how the golden oak looked so much like the color of Marshall's burnished skin. She moved to one of the big windows and stood gazing out at the green expanse of lawn that rolled away from the building to the parking lot beyond.

Large hands settled on her shoulders and Jessie's heart surged joyfully just before a masculine voice asked, "Why so pensive, Jessie? Have a boring weekend?"

Jessie shrugged the hands away and side-stepped around the man. "Hello, Pete."

The science teacher shook his hand as though he'd scorched it. "I see the ice princess is in rare form this morning," he said. "What's the matter, did someone try to get a goodnight kiss?"

"Grow up."

"Oh, I already have, Jess. The question is, when are you going to try it? You go around here like Miss Untouchable."

Jessie waved a dismissive hand. "Forget it. Just leave me alone, will you?"

Pete spun on his heel and crossed the library in long furious strides. Jessie knew he wouldn't be back. The first bell rang and she turned to her desk to check the day's schedule.

The perfume of roses hung heavily in the air. Jessie decided she'd divide the bouquet, leaving a dozen here in the living room and putting the other dozen in her bedroom. Or maybe a few in a bud vase on the kitchen table. The flowers had been delivered shortly after she arrived home this afternoon with a card that said simply, *I love you. Marsh.* An extravagant, but sweet gesture.

Jessie lifted a stem from the vase and fingered the petals before inhaling its fragrance. She sighed. She missed him already. The telephone rang and she jumped for it.

"Hello?"

"Hi," Ellen greeted her. "I'm ready for the next installment."

As was often the case, Jessie had no idea what her friend meant. "What installment?"

"Of the latest love story, *The Lawman and the Librarian*, of course."

Jessie sat in shocked silence, the receiver clutched to her ear.

"Jessie?"

"How did you know?" she asked dully, not really wanting to know.

"Then it's true?" Ellen sounded so excited.

"Yes!"

"Jessie, what's wrong? You sound madder than a wet hen."

"You don't think I should be?" She was seething.

"Maybe we'd better start over. We must be talking about two different things," Ellen said soothingly.

"What are *you* talking about?"

"Love. What are *you* talking about?"

"Conquests, and men who boast about them."

"You've lost me," Ellen confessed.

"Okay," Jessie sighed, "back to the beginning. What have you heard that prompted this conversation?"

"Mike called a little while ago to tell me that

before he left for the valley, Marsh asked him to look after you."

Jessie sat in silence for a moment. "That's all? I don't follow."

"Jessie! The only reason a man would ask his friend to 'look after' a woman is because he's in love with her. It's sure not because you're in danger of being ambushed by the Dalton Gang."

Awash with relief, Jessie giggled, "No, but there's always the Swartz Gang."

"What? Oh, the boys in the truck. No, I don't think that's what he had in mind."

"I know."

"Then it *is* true—you're really seeing Marsh now?"

Jessie closed her eyes and smiled. "Yes, I guess you could say that."

Ellen's voice was hopeful. "Do you think he's the one, Jessie?"

Jessie sighed and lifted the rose to her nostrils again. "Yes," she answered quietly. "I think he's the one, El."

"I'm glad. I like him."

"Me too."

Jessie asked about the baby and they talked for a few more minutes before hanging up. After that, she wandered through the house, wondering what to do with the empty evening that stretched before her. She didn't want to work in the yard for fear of missing Marshall if he called.

At supper time, Jessie fixed herself a sandwich, added cheese, crackers, and an apple to her plate, and carried it into the front room to eat. She switched on the news, something she rarely did, just in case, then realized that Marshall wouldn't even get to his destination until sometime tonight, let alone have time to catch his quarry. Ellen had said Mike talked to him a little after ten o'clock this morning, so he hadn't gotten out of town much before noon.

Jessie sat distractedly brushing her hair. Almost ten o'clock and still no word from Marshall. She'd taken a quick bath, leaving the door open so she could hear the telephone, but it hadn't made a sound. She'd locked the house up earlier and Nan and Sheba were already bedded down, the dog beside her bed, the cat on it. She might as well turn out the light and go to sleep.

The telephone rang, startling Jessie and eliciting a growl from Nan. She flew across the room and grabbed the receiver.

"Hello?"

"I love you."

Jessie closed her eyes against the sweet pain that his husky voice evoked. "The flowers are beautiful."

"So are you."

"Where are you?"

"In Alice."

"Where's that?"

"A little west of Corpus."

"Is that where you'll be?"

"No, I'm just stopping here for the night. I just got in."

"You didn't make very good time."

"Jess, you don't go barreling down the highway towing a horse behind you. I also stopped a couple of times to walk him. I'll need him ready to travel as soon as I get there tomorrow. Besides, by the time I left the office, drove back out to Jim's, hitched the trailer, loaded horse and gear, and grabbed something to eat, it was nearly noon."

"You took Scout with you?"

"Yep. We'll have to cover some areas that are better traveled by horseback."

"Oh. Where will you be tomorrow?"

"I'm headed for Rio Grande City, and from there we'll play it by ear." Before she could ask, Marshall added, "That's upriver from McAllen."

"I'm sorry, I didn't mean to sound like I'm keeping track of you."

"I know." His voice warm and soft, Marshall continued, "I like the thought though, that a beautiful woman is concerned about where I am and what I'm doing."

"And whether you're safe."

"And whether I'm safe. I miss you, Jess."

"Oh, Marsh, I miss you too. I'd given up on your calling tonight and I felt so let down."

"Really?"

"Really."

"I guess I'd better warn you now then, this is probably the last you'll hear from me for several days. But don't worry. Just keep in mind that old saying about no news being good news. Mike would hear if there's a problem."

Jessie swallowed her sudden tears and bit her lip.

"Jess, are you there?"

"Ye—yes, I'm here."

"What were you doing when I called?"

"Brushing my hair."

Marshall groaned. "I wish I were there."

"So do I."

"Well, I guess I'd better go. Goodnight, sweetheart."

Jessie squeezed her eyes shut and tears leaked out the corners. She didn't want him to hang up, to sever this last connection between them for who knew how long.

"Jess?"

The tenderness in his voice undid her. Jessie sobbed into the phone, unable to hold it back any longer.

"Honey, don't," Marshall murmured, "please, don't. I love you."

"Oh, Marsh," Jessie choked, "I love you too." She drew a shuddering breath. "I love you too, and I don't know what to do."

"Jess." He breathed her name in wonder. This was the first time she'd spoken the words.

"What do I do now?" she whispered.

"Wait for me, Jess, can you do that?"

"I . . . I don . . . don't have any choice, do . . . do I?"

"Shhh, baby, it'll be all right. I'll contact you whenever I can. Just remember I love you and I'm coming back for you."

"I love you."

"I know."

Jessie gave a broken chuckle. "Egotistical gringo."

"Sassy Injun."

"Be careful."

"I will."

"Promise?"

"I have too much to lose now not to."

Jessie knew in advance that she wouldn't hear from him, so Tuesday and Wednesday weren't too bad. But by Thursday, she felt completely at loose ends. After school, she headed to Ellen's.

"Jessie! What a nice surprise. Come in."

Ellen stepped back from the door, the baby cradled in her arms. Jessie followed her into the house and held up a grocery bag.

"Whatcha got there?"

"Something for us and something for Michelle." Jessie pulled a colorful plastic rattle from the bag and shook it. "For Michelle." Then lifted out a half-gallon container of pecan praline ice cream. "For us."

"Alll riiight," Ellen cheered.

While Ellen tucked her daughter into a padded baby carrier and set it on the kitchen table, Jessie got out the bowls and spoons.

"How about that, Michelle," Ellen cooed, "this is your very first 'girl talk' session."

Jessie laughed and pushed a bowl towards her friend. They ate in silence for a moment, then Ellen cocked her head to one side. "Okay, so talk."

Jessie continued to eat. "About what?"

"About whatever caused you to buy the ice cream."

Ellen knew her too well. They'd done this for years. Whenever one was upset or needed help with a problem, or just a sympathetic ear, she would carry a carton of ice cream to the other's

house and over bowls of double chocolate or pecan praline, they'd hash it out.

"I miss Marshall," Jessie confessed.

Ellen's spoon stopped halfway to her mouth.
She carefully lowered it back to the bowl. "You
met him a month ago, he's only been gone three
days, and you miss him?"

Jessie nodded miserably.

"I don't understand. From what you've told me
you only went out . . ."

"We spent last weekend together," Jessie interrupted.

"*All* weekend?"

"He took me horseback riding after school Friday, then he came over Saturday and helped with
chores and grilled hot dogs, then he came over
Sunday and we drove to Brenham," Jessie recited
in a rush.

"Oh," Ellen murmured, backing down from her
original impression. She reached over and
grasped her friend's hand. "Oh, Jessie. I don't
know whether to be happy for you or to cry."

Jessie raised tearful eyes and chuckled. "Neither do I."

"What now?"

"I don't know. He said he loves me, and to
wait for him."

"And?"

"And I love him, El, I'm sure I do."

"But you didn't know it would hurt."

"No, you never told me about that part."

Ellen grinned and squeezed Jessie's hand. "I did so! Don't you remember how many times I'd be the one carrying the ice cream because one guy or another had made me miserable?"

"But this is different. We aren't kids anymore."

"No, we're not, and this is for real. But that only means that there's more at stake here and when it hurts, it hurts more deeply."

Jessie sighed and nodded as she stirred her ice cream into mush.

"He's a good man, Jessie. Mike says so. He'll be worth the wait, you'll see."

The weekend came and Jessie tried to stay busy. She hung Marshall's wind chime in a corner of the front yard, where they could hear it on the porch. She pruned the shrubbery and planted caladium bulbs. She painted the picnic table and the barbecue grill. Sunday afternoon she drove over to see her mother and stayed for supper. But nothing helped. Marshall remained foremost in her thoughts.

Monday evening she called Ellen to ask if Mike had mentioned anything.

"Just a minute, I'll ask if they've heard from him."

"Ellen, no!"

"Why not?"

"You know how men are. I don't want Marshall to think I'm checking up on him."

"He wouldn't have to know."

"And I don't want to start any gossip up there."

"You have a point. Okay, I'll keep my ears open."

"Thanks, El. Bye."

Jessie got out a state roadmap and located Rio Grande City and Alice. She folded the map so that the Rio Grande valley was displayed and tacked it to the small cork board in the kitchen. A silly gesture, but knowing where the places were made him seem a little closer.

The next morning, Billy Stovall was waiting for Jessie on the school steps. "I wanted to thank you for letting me work off the cost of the book, Miss Holgrave."

"I'm glad I could help, Billy. An honest man who takes his responsibilities seriously is hard to find these days."

Billy shrugged and scuffed his shoe against a spot on the pavement, trying to rub it away.

"Is there something else I could help with?"

Billy glanced up, then away. "Well, maybe. That is, I was hopin' . . ."

"Come on in," Jessie said as she invited him to follow her. In the library, she dropped her things on her desk and sat down, motioning Billy to the chair by her desk. "Okay, what's up?"

"Well, I was just wondering if you could help me with an idea for a summer job. I'm not old enough to get hired on at the grocery store or the fast-food places."

"What about doing yard work?"

"I've been doing that for the past three summers, but now my brother Donny's old enough so I gave him my customers."

"I see. That's very generous of you."

"Not really. I'd like a chance to make more money than that."

Jessie didn't ask for what. She knew his earnings went to help with the family's expenses. Suddenly, she smiled.

"Billy, do you like horses?"

"Yes, ma'am."

"Enough to clean stalls?"

"Heck, Miss Holgrave, manure washes right off."

Jessie laughed. "It certainly does, doesn't it? Let me call a friend of mine, and if he's needing help, we'll go over Saturday and talk to him. Mention it to your parents first, though. I'll talk to them about it when I pick you up."

"Yes, ma'am! Thank you, Miss Holgrave, thanks a lot!"

"Hold onto your thanks until I see if Jim can use you," Jessie called, but Billy was already out the door.

That afternoon, Jessie found a florist's delivery van in front of her house when she got home. A young woman in jeans and tee shirt stood just outside the gate. She turned as Jessie pulled her car to a stop.

"Jess Holgrave?"

"Yes."

"Thank goodness!" The girl gave a relieved sigh. "I didn't know what to do about the *Beware of Dog* sign. I yelled but no one came."

"The sign's for real, but I left the dog in the house this morning," Jessie explained as she signed for the large vase of roses.

"Well, have a nice day. Looks like someone is thinking of you," the girl quipped as she trotted around the van.

Jessie resisted opening the card until she'd carried the arrangement inside. She knew who'd sent it: The girl had asked for "Jess." The card read *I miss you terribly, and I still love you. Marsh.* The roses, heavily interspersed with baby's breath, both lifted and weighed her heart.

Though thrilled to know he was thinking of her, Jessie missed Marshall so much she wanted to cry. She wrapped her arms around the vase and hugged it to her, but the cold, slender container did nothing to alleviate the ache left by Marshall's absence. Only his solid body could fill that void. She set the flowers on the table with a sigh, then went to change clothes.

Knowing he'd be busy, Jessie waited until evening to call Jim.

Jessie glanced at the boy beside her. Billy sat straight in the seat, his eyes glued on the road ahead. She could tell he was trying to hide his excitement. His mother had reluctantly agreed to let him come for this interview. Jessie had told the Stovalls that Jim would probably want Billy to stay at the ranch through the week, as that would be easier for all concerned, and would bring him home for weekends. Mrs. Stovall had balked at that, but the exhilaration in Billy's face had won her over. She knew it would be a great opportunity for her son, especially when Jessie explained that she herself had started with Jim at about the same age.

Jessie gave a short beep on the car's horn as she pulled up next to the stables. By the time she and Billy were out of the car, Jim had emerged, a big smile on his face.

"Jessie, girl, how are you?"

Jessie returned Jim's hug. "Fine, thanks. I've brought your new wrangler."

Jim looked at the thin boy standing nervously

before him and smiled gently as he held out his hand. "Wrangler?"

Billy shook the proffered hand solemnly. "I'll need to start out as a stable hand until I get the chance to learn," he explained.

"Fair enough," Jim nodded. "How about I show you around while Jessie goes down to the house to see her cousin Nonnie?"

"Yes, sir." Billy looked up at Jessie. "Guess I'll see you in a bit, Miss Holgrave?"

Jessie smiled her reassurance to the boy. "You men will come down when you've finished the tour?"

"Sure thing," Jim answered. "Once the boy tastes Nonnie's cookies, he'll be sure to take the job."

An hour later, Jim called the house from the stable before they started down, giving Jessie and Nonnie a chance to carry lemonade and a platter of cookies out onto the wide front porch before he and Billy got there. He introduced the lad to his wife and watched surreptitiously as Billy devoured the cookies, but with appropriate manners. When Nonnie took over, asking Billy to give her a hand carrying things back to the kitchen, Jim turned his attention to Jessie.

"Has he ever been in trouble?"

"Not that I know of, Jim. He comes from honest, hardworking people, but as I told you, they don't have much."

Jim nodded. "What about him staying during the week?"

"His mother was understandably hesitant about that, but his parents both see it as a good opportunity, so she agreed."

"He's too young to put out with the men. He can use Bud's old room."

Jessie smiled to herself. She knew darn well that Jim never intended to put a thirteen-year-old boy in the bunkhouse. Even if he had entertained the thought, Nonnie would have disabused him of the notion in no time. They'd only had one child, much to their regret, and were notorious for trying to take in everyone else's. Their son Bud, a lawyer now, didn't get up to see his parents very often, and remained unmarried at this point, so there weren't any grandchildren to dote on.

No, Billy wouldn't be in the bunkhouse. He'd be cosseted by the couple, who would look upon him as a foster child, just as they had Jessie for so many years.

"Heard from Marsh?"

Jim's voice intruded on Jessie's reverie, the subject startling her. "Marsh?" She feigned ignorance. "Oh, you mean Marshall Abbott?"

Jim snorted. "Don't give me that, you know darn well who I mean, girl."

Jessie blushed. "He's in the Rio Grande valley, I believe."

"I know where he went, Jessie, I helped him load his blamed horse! Surely he's called you. Is he okay?"

"I haven't talked to him in a week and a half, but he, ah, sent me some flowers on Tuesday," Jessie reluctantly admitted, "so I'm assuming he's all right."

"Flowers, huh?"

"Don't start on me, Jim."

"Why? Don't you like him? The boy's nuts about you."

"He told you that?"

"Yep. The day you two came riding. Worst case of love at first sight I've ever heard tell of."

"Jim . . ."

"You could do a lot worse, Jessie. He's a fine man, and he's not ashamed to say he loves you."

Jessie dropped her gaze to her lap. "I know."

Jim's eyebrows shot up at her tone. "Oh? And?"

"And I love him, too."

"Hallelujah!" Jim leaped from his chair and pulled Jessie up for a bear hug. "I'm sure glad to hear it, honey. We'd begun to think you'd never find a man you'd trust. Nonnie's gonna be tickled pink."

Jessie laughed. "I'm pretty pleased about it myself."

Chapter Nine

The telephone rang and Jessie rushed to answer it.

"Where have you been? I've been trying to get you all day!"

"Excuse me? What number were you calling, sir?"

"Jess!"

"Mr. Abbott, is that you?"

Marshall chuckled ruefully. "I love you."

"That's better. I love you too. Are you all right, where are you, and when are you coming home?"

At Jessie's barrage of questions, Marshall laughed openly, a warm, full-throated sound. "Man, I've missed you."

"Me, too, but you didn't answer me."

"I'm fine. Hot, tired, dirty, but fine. I'm still in the valley, at a truck stop in the middle of nowhere, and I don't know when I'll be back."

"Oh, Marsh."

"I know. But wait for me, honey. Please."

"I'm not going anywhere," Jess answered softly.

"Then how come I couldn't get you all day? I thought Saturday was when you did your housework."

Jessie smiled at the petulance in his voice. "I went out to Jim's. He asked about you."

"Next time you see him say hi for me and tell him Scout is doing fine."

"Okay."

"Did you ride?"

"No, I took him a prospective stable hand, and visited with Nonnie while Jim conducted the interview."

"Oh?" The line was silent while Marshall tried to phrase his next question. "Where, ah, where did you meet this guy?" he asked casually.

He didn't fool Jessie. "Oh, he hangs around sometimes, waiting for me at school."

"Oh." A prolonged silence followed.

"His name is Billy Stovall, and he has the most beautiful brown eyes . . ."

They couldn't be as beautiful as yours, Marshall thought miserably.

". . . and he's thirteen years old, and is finishing the seventh grade."

"What?"

Marsh sounded dazed and Jessie chuckled. "He's a boy from my school, Marsh. He needs a summer job and I thought he and Jim would be perfect for each other."

Marshall released a long sigh of relief. *Evil woman, she did that on purpose!* "Did Jim hire him?" He wouldn't let Jess know she'd got him on that one.

"Yes, he'll start the first Monday after school is out. He'll be staying with Jim and Nonnie during the week and going home on weekends. He's so excited he didn't stop talking all the way home."

"That's nice."

Suddenly aware that Marshall didn't really want to hear about Billy, Jessie finished, "Anyway, that's where I was. I'm sorry that I put you to extra trouble."

"You didn't put me to any trouble, Jess," he replied warmly, his voice low enough to make her insides tremble. "I just got worried when I couldn't reach you."

"I'm sorry. But as you can tell, I'm fine."

Marshall gave a short bark of laughter. "You're more than fine, lady, and your physical well-being isn't all I worried about."

"You've lost me."

"Oh, come on, Jess," he growled, "I could just picture you with one of Jim's hands, riding across the pastures, or with one of the guys who teaches at your school, going to the museums."

"Marshall Abbott, I told you I love you and you still thought I was out with another man?" Jessie's voice rose in volume. "I can't believe it!"

"Jess, calm down, I'm sorry. I really didn't mean it that way."

"Then exactly how did you mean it?"

"I . . . I don't know. I'm just missing you so much, and I . . . I guess I thought that maybe I'd imagined it all. What happened between us, I mean. God knows I can't understand what a woman like you would see in me."

"A woman like me?" Jessie asked suspiciously.

"Yeah, a woman like you." Marshall's voice dropped again. "Beautiful, educated, amusing, intelligent, and sexy as all get out."

"Flatterer," Jessie whispered.

Marshall groaned. "Jess, I wish you were here with me."

"So do I, darling, so do I."

That night Jessie's dreams were definitely of a romantic nature, if somewhat offbeat. Marshall came striding to her across a mist-shrouded pasture wearing only jeans and boots, an oversized

Ranger's badge pinned to the impressive mus-
culature of his bare chest. In the morning Jessie
giggled and winced as she remembered it.

Monday marked the beginning of their third
week apart, and Marshall again sent flowers. This
time Jessie opened her door for the delivery of a
decorative basket filled with a colorful spring
bouquet. The card read, *Don't forget me. You're
never out of my thoughts. Love, Marsh.*

On Wednesday, she notified the teachers that
all library books had to be returned by the following Friday, giving the children ten days to
comply. Only three weeks of school remained before the summer break.

Thursday evening she sat in front of the television, eating pasta salad while she watched the
news. The broadcast was leading into a commer-
cial and she rose to carry her dish to the kitchen,
but froze in place when the commentator issued
the teaser for the second half the show.

"When we return, we'll have exclusive footage
of an operation in the Rio Grande valley. A cit-
izen filmed Texas Rangers and federal immigration agents in a rare joint effort as they dragged
undocumented workers from a warehouse, kicking and beating them in the process."

Jessie sank back to the couch, the dish forgotten in her hand. A seemingly endless number of
products flitted across the screen, promising

everything from happy pets to the mate of your dreams. But none of it registered with Jessie. She sat, biting her lip, barely daring to breathe for fear of missing the upcoming report.

The newscaster returned to the screen, his expression hard, his voice somber. "In footage that may rival that of the Rodney King arrest in political repercussions, an unnamed tourist captured Texas Rangers and federal border patrol agents at work. The following is graphic, so parents may wish to send young children from the room." He paused dramatically, then continued. "Reportedly, the Immigration Service and the Texas Rangers became temporary partners in a late-night assault on a warehouse in Starr County. The Rangers were tracking smugglers who bring undocumented workers into Texas. The federal agents, of course, were looking for the illegal aliens. As you can see from this video, it had all the earmarks of a military campaign."

A dim image filled the television screen, showing what appeared to be a corrugated tin building with high windows. Yard lights mounted at the corners made circles of illumination on the ground. Suddenly a dark-clad figure ran to the building and pressed itself against the wall, inching stealthily to the nearest window. Another figure followed, and another.

Jessie watched, spellbound, as the first figure

raised his arm and motioned to his unseen forces. Within seconds, the building was surrounded by the dark figures, identified by reflective lettering on their jackets. Jessie's heart stopped when she realized that among the rush of men were several wearing Stetson hats.

When her heart resumed pumping, it pounded so hard that she couldn't hear the newsman. His voice remained an unintelligible accompaniment to the drama unfolding on the screen.

With a shout, the law enforcement officers broke through the doors and poured into the building. The few men who were desperate enough to try to escape out the windows were quickly subdued by the armed agents awaiting them. The camera zoomed in on agents throwing men to the ground, holding them with booted feet on their necks as their arms were twisted behind them so their hands could be secured with plastic wraps.

One young man broke free, but froze when a warning gunshot split the air. He dropped to his knees, his arms raised in the air. When he'd been secured, an agent nudged him back toward the others. The man stumbled but remained on his feet until he reached the group and the agent urged him to the ground. The agent knelt immediately and lashed the young man's ankles together as well, presumably because he'd run.

Jessie hugged herself tightly, marginally aware that she felt chilled, her mouth dry, her throat tight.

Behind the crowd of federal agents and aliens, Jessie saw two cowboy-hatted figures exiting the building, dragging a man between them. The camera zoomed in on the thrashing figure and the newsman's voice penetrated Jessie's consciousness.

". . . and here is the footage that is certain to raise questions regarding whether the methods of the Texas Rangers have indeed come in line with the twenty-first century."

Jessie watched dumbfounded as one Ranger kicked the prostrate man in the midsection. He grunted and curled reflexively.

The television station turned up the sound on the videotape. A man's voice growled, "You lousy wetback, you think you can open a highway for whoever wants to come into this country, don't you?"

Jessie's breath caught in her throat as the tall Ranger dragged his captive up by the shirt, then raised his fist. The film ended abruptly as Jessie's heart stopped again. This time she knew it was forever. She knew it would never beat again. The man abusing the unarmed, dark-skinned prisoner was Marshall Abbott.

Jessie lurched to her feet, her stomach painfully knotted. She barely made it to the bathroom in time to lose her dinner. She remained on her knees, panting, as waves of nausea broke over her. Finally, the cramping stopped. She rose unsteadily to her feet to rinse her mouth and to wipe her face with a cool washcloth. Reaction set in with uncontrollable tremors as she stumbled to her room to collapse on her bed.

Curled in a fetal position, much as the prisoner had been, she stared at a smudge on the far wall while tears coursed unheeded down her face. Funny, she hadn't noticed that spot before. She'd have to get a sponge and wash it off. Yes, that's what she would have to do. She'd go into the kitchen and get a sponge. She'd dampen it under the faucet, but just a little. Too much water and it would run down the wall. She'd get her spray cleaner and spray the spot then. . . . then . . .

A low moan escaped her lips. It grew until it became an eerie howl of soul-shattering pain, a primitive wail of heartsick sorrow, a mindless protest of life's unbelievable horrors.

On the porch, Nan began barking frantically, totally out of character for a Chow. He pawed at the front door, whimpering and howling, but Jessie couldn't hear him. Turned inward to the yawning chasm where her heart had been only a short hour ago, she couldn't hear anything in the outside world.

The ringing telephone woke her. Jessie glanced at the clock: it was nearly ten-thirty. Her head pounded and her eyes were swollen. Her stomach hurt. The phone kept ringing. She sat up and eased her legs over the side of the bed.

Ignoring the telephone, she went to the door to let Sheba and Nan in, then automatically turned to the kitchen to feed them. Nan, however, just gave his dish a quick sniff and followed his mistress as she wandered back to her room. When Jessie dropped again to the edge of her bed and began massaging her temples with her fingertips, Nan laid his chin on her knee and studied her from sad brown eyes. His ears drooped back, letting her know he was bothered.

"Poor Nan, I forgot about you, didn't I?" Jessie stroked his head and the dog gave his tail a half-hearted wag. "I'm sorry Nan," she whispered, "I'm sorry, I'm so sorry."

The tears began again. Nan jumped onto the bed, pushing his head under her arm and into Jessie's lap in an attempt to comfort her. She curled her body over the dog and hugged him to her, pouring out her grief into his thick black coat.

Again, the ringing telephone woke Jessie. She sat up with a start at the realization that sunlight streamed through the windows. Blocking out the repetitive shrilling in the next room, she quickly washed her face and began pulling on her clothes. The telephone fell silent and she relaxed her shoulders, unaware until that moment that she'd tensed her body against the unknown caller.

She hurried to let Nan outside and filled bowls with pet food. With no time to make coffee, she grabbed a glass of orange juice and carried it back to the bathroom to sip on while she did her makeup. As she twisted her hair into a coil, the telephone sounded again. She couldn't dodge it forever, she supposed.

"Hello!"

"Jessie?" Ellen sounded surprised at the brusque salutation. "This is Ellen, I—"

"Ellen, I can't talk now, I overslept. Catch you later, okay?"

Jessie hung up quickly and took a step back from the phone, as though it were hot to the touch. Tears blurred her vision and the fingers she pressed to her lips trembled. She stumbled back to her room to finish getting ready for work.

In a state of distraction, Jessie managed to get through the day by blocking out the previous night's newscast.

The telephone began ringing within moments of her arrival, so she unplugged it. Life had no intention of letting her off that easily. She opened the paper she'd not had time for that morning to find a bold headline proclaiming *Hispanic Leaders Up In Arms*. The subheading read, *Beating by Rangers Galvanizes Mexican-American Community*. She threw the newspaper into the kitchen garbage and got a chilled can of cream soda from the refrigerator.

Wandering to her bedroom, Nan close by her side, Jessie sat on the foot of the bed and kicked off her shoes. She sighed and the dog whimpered and gently pawed her leg.

Jessie stroked his silky head. "What's the matter, boy, am I upsetting you? Don't worry, I'll be okay." Jessie sighed, then vowed, "I don't know when, but I will be okay."

Changing into jeans, she went out to work in the yard, determined to put the whole episode behind her. She wasn't ready yet to deal with how thoroughly Marshall had deceived her. She'd thought he believed in justice for all—no matter what their ethnic background.

A consummate actor, he'd gotten past her defenses with relative ease. How he must have gloried in his conquest, knowing all along he personified the very type of man Jessie abhorred! A pain settled in the region of her heart. No, she wasn't ready to deal with any of that just yet.

She took up a broom to sweep the patio, but soon found herself staring at the grill, picturing Marshall there, cooking hot dogs. Shaking her head to dispel the image, she walked around the side of the house to sweep the walk and porch. But a breeze stirred the wind chime, and its tinkling music conjured up Marshall's image on the porch swing, long legs stretched out before him.

"I'm losing my mind," she muttered softly.

A car turned into Jessie's street and she ran for the back yard. She didn't want to see anyone. She heard the car door slam, then a minute later a second one did likewise. Someone rang the doorbell. Nan barked, but only once. The caller then began pounding on the door, but Nan stayed quiet. It had to be someone he knew.

"Jessie? Jessie, I know you're in there. Open up!" More pounding. "Jessie, open this door!" Pound, pound, pound. "Jessica Bluefeather Holgrave, you open this door right now!"

Jessie sighed and opened the screen door to go through and let Ellen in the front.

"It's about time!" Ellen snapped as she juggled her wailing infant's plastic carrier, a diaper bag, and her purse. "You made me scare the baby with all that racket."

"Ellen, please, I don't . . ."

"Take her," Ellen ordered as she pushed the carrier at Jessie.

Jessie obeyed, setting the contraption on the coffee table and extracting the distressed baby. Tucking Michelle into her shoulder, Jessie patted the tiny back and crooned softly into the sweet-scented little ear. Michelle quieted almost at once.

"Get in here," Ellen ordered from the kitchen, her voice sharp and still very annoyed.

Jessie stepped through the door and Ellen pointed to a kitchen chair. "Sit!"

Nan obeyed immediately, but Jessie hesitated. The table was set with napkins, spoons, and two huge bowls of fudge ripple ice cream.

"Ellen, I don't want . . ."

"Right now, Jessie, I don't care what you want," Ellen interrupted sternly. Her voice finally softened as she added, "It's what you need, Jessie. I saw the ten o'clock news and knew you did too when you wouldn't answer the phone. Talk to me, Jessie."

Jessie slid into a chair; Michelle still cuddled close.

"Mike asked me to tell you something," Ellen told her as she took the facing chair. "He doesn't know what's going on, but he wants you to know that he trusts Marsh and that you shouldn't believe everything you see."

Jessie shook her head slowly. "I can understand not believing everything you hear, but that video left little room for interpretation, El."

"I know it did, but that's just not like Marsh, you *know* it isn't, Jessie."

"Not like the Marsh he showed to us, you

mean. I saw him, El! I heard him! There's no
doubt at all in my mind that it was Marshall Abbott on last night's news, beating a helpless man
senseless. And if you'd be truly honest, you'd
admit it too."

Ellen nodded glumly. "It did look that way,
didn't it?"

Jessie choked back a sob and whispered, "Oh,
Ellen, how could he?"

"I don't know, Jessie, I just don't know."

Jessie closed her eyes and rocked gently back
and forth on the kitchen chair, caressing the small
fuzzy head on her shoulder with her cheek. A
single tear slid down her face.

They sat in silence awhile, poking and prod-
ding at their bowls of ice cream, but neither eating much. Michelle began stirring on Jessie's
shoulder and Ellen checked her watch. "Feeding
time." Then she frowned and looked again.
"Mike said he'd call me here at four to be sure
everything was okay. He must have gotten busy."

Jessie had lowered the infant to her arms and
gently ran a fingertip around the baby's face.
"Hmm? Oh. I unplugged the phone when I got
home from school."

"Why?"

"It kept ringing."

"And you didn't want to talk to me," Ellen
accused.

Jessie shrugged one shoulder. "You or who-ever."

Ellen shook her head and rose from the table. "I'll be right back."

Jessie followed a moment later and asked, "Has he heard anything?"

Ellen shook her head and said into the mouth-piece, "She's as well as can be expected. Yes, I'll tell her. Bye, honey." Ellen hung up and turned to her friend. "Mike said to tell you to keep the faith."

"How much does Mike know? I mean about me and—" Jessie broke off. It hurt too much to even say his name.

"Only that Marsh is interested in you, and that you've gone out with him. Of course that in itself tells Mike quite a lot. He knows you pretty well by now."

Ellen unfastened her shirt and put the baby to her breast. The ancient rite of motherhood stung Jessie and she turned away to stare out a window, her hands jammed into her back pockets. "Oh God," she murmured, "how could it all go so wrong?"

When Ellen left, Jessie threw a few things into an overnight bag, poured out extra food for Sheba, and loaded Nan into the car. She'd spend the weekend at Jim and Nonnie's. No, she thought, that wouldn't help a bit.

She'd go to her brother Jaquin's cabin on the lake, that's what. The last she'd heard, he'd be working outside of Tyler for at least another month, so he wouldn't be using it.

Jessie stopped in the little town of Pinehurst for a few groceries and a paperback book. Maybe she could lose herself between the pages for a weekend. The evening news played on a small television set by the cash register of the gas station/bait shop/grocery store. The heavyset man behind the counter swore softly, "Doggone if it don't look like that Ranger's fried his own tail."

Woodenly, Jessie set her purchases down before him.

"Evening, little lady, how y'doin'? This be all for ya?"

Jessie nodded and pulled out her wallet. "Darn shame 'bout that mess over by San Isidro, ain't it?" he continued conversationally. "They had no call t'beat up on those boys that way."

Jessie swallowed and nodded dumbly. Privately, she thought the proprietor, seeing a dark-skinned customer, was just looking after his business interests.

Chapter Ten

Tilting the chair back on two legs, Jessie propped her heels on the porch railing and took a long drink from the chilled bottle of vegetable juice.

Nan ran past her, chasing a squirrel up a tree, then darted down to the lake's edge before galloping back to Jessie's side, his tongue lolling. She patted his head and he took off again, this time after a blue jay.

Daylight faded and chimney swifts sailed overhead, little chattering chirps announcing their passing. For a moment, Jessie watched the ballet as the small birds wheeled and dove, chasing insects through the lowering dusk. Nan came charging back, then dropped in an exhausted heap next to his mistress. He yawned, stretched, and promptly went to sleep.

Jessie envied him. There'd be little sleep for her again tonight. She'd only dozed fitfully last night, between crying jags and nightmares.

A cool breeze blew from across the lake, smoothing a tendril of hair back from her cheek like the touch of a hand. *Like the touch of Marshall's hand.* With a strangled sob, Jessie leaped to her feet and flung the bottle with all her might. Grimly satisfied by the sound of the glass shattering against a tree, Jessie made a mental note to clean up the shards in the morning. She sighed and turned towards the door, snapping her fingers for Nan to follow.

Inside the darkened cabin, she hesitated, wondering if she should eat something. She couldn't remember whether she'd eaten today or not. It didn't matter; she wasn't hungry.

The cedar A-frame cabin had a private bedroom and bath downstairs, as well as a large gathering room, a half bath, a laundry, and a kitchen. But Jessie chose the sleeping loft, dragging her weary body up the narrow staircase. She positioned a foam mattress so that she could see through the railing, out the tall windows and over the lake. The red and green lights of a boat passed by and on the far shore, lights twinkled from houses, cabins, and campers. Nan began to snore, the sound oddly comforting.

The high pitched whine of a boat motor woke Jessie. She frowned and rubbed her eyes, momentarily disoriented, then glanced down. She wasn't surprised to find herself still fully dressed. What amazed her was that she'd slept. Thinking sleep unlikely, she hadn't bothered to disrobe, expecting to be up prowling the cabin during the night.

The sun hadn't yet risen, but its light already illuminated the morning. She stood and stretched, then jogged down the stairs to let Nan out. Before showering, she filled the electric coffee maker and plugged it in. By the time she finished in the bathroom, the aroma of coffee would fill the small house. Smiling at that thought, she pulled a change of clothes from her bag.

A short while later, she padded barefoot onto the porch, a mug of coffee in one hand, her father's guitar in the other. The birds were awake now and filling the trees with song. Once the sun warmed the air, jet skis would rip through the serenity with the finesse of a buzz saw. Weekenders would launch boats from the public ramp and private docks, pulling water skiers or just racing each other. Until then, Jessie intended to enjoy the relative peace.

She propped one ankle on her knee and snuggled the old guitar comfortably into place. Idly strumming chords, she let her gaze drift over the lake, where the sun would soon make its appearance. She loved this time of morning. Without thought or intent, the fingers of her left hand formed the chords for her right hand to strum. Before long, she found herself playing one of her father's favorite pieces, *Blue Spanish Eyes*. It seemed only natural to follow with his favorite hymn. She hummed along, drawing comfort from the easy, flowing melody of *Amazing Grace*. After that, she again strummed idly, but memories of her father opened the door for memories of another, more recent loss, and the chords took on the melancholy sounds of the minor keys.

Tears formed on her lids and Jessie muttered to herself, "Oh, why not," and played one of her own favorite oldies, *Vaya Con Dios*. Go with God. Marshall had hurt her, hurt her badly with his deception, but because she'd loved him she wanted him safe. Safe so *I* could kill him, she thought grimly.

She sang the song through softly to herself, but when she came to the last verse, the one about parting, she couldn't go on. Tears ran down her cheeks as she continued to play the piece to its end, but her trembling lips couldn't form the words. The final chord echoed in the morning air.

Jessie drew a shuddering breath and reached for her cup of coffee. Nan came bounding through the underbrush, tongue lolling, tail wagging, coat absolutely soaked. He'd been swimming in the lake and wanted to share that news with his mistress.

"Nan, no! Don't you dare!"

Jessie squealed and jumped to her feet, but not in time to keep the dog from doing what dogs do. He shook himself vigorously, giving Jessie her second shower of the morning.

Heading inside, Jessie stripped off her splattered sweatshirt and pulled a clean t-shirt over her head, then curled up in the big papasan chair by the windows. Morning sun poured in the front of the cabin now, and she settled with the book she'd bought and another cup of coffee. For the rest of the weekend, she'd lose herself in someone else's troubles, secure in the knowledge that by the end of the story, everything would be all right.

It was nearly ten o'clock when Jessie pulled up to her dark house Sunday night and she realized that unconsciously, she'd planned it that way. If it hadn't been for the need to get up early Monday for work, she might have stayed later—or not come back at all. Still, she felt better than she had a couple of days ago.

The telephone began ringing before she'd even had a chance to empty her overnight bag. Jessie considered ignoring it, unplugging it, or maybe getting an answering machine so she could screen her calls. She'd never before wanted to avoid the phone. Not before Marshall, anyway. She sighed and picked up the receiver.

"Hello," she answered flatly.

"Jessie, I've been worried sick, are you all right?"

"I'm fine, Ellen, I just went up to the lake for the weekend. I guess I should have let you know. I'm sorry."

Ellen breathed a great sigh of relief. "Yes, you should have," she admonished, but without heat. "I figured you probably just wanted to get away, but I wasn't sure. Did it help?"

"I think it did. I'm still hurting, but not as badly. Look Ellen, I'm sorry I worried you, but I'm bushed. Can we talk later?"

"Of course. Get your beauty rest and give me a call, okay?"

"Okay. Thanks, El."

Jessie hung up and turned from the telephone, paused, and turned back. She bit her lower lip as she studied it a moment, then sighed and un-plugged the cord.

She'd begin her inventory with the reference books, encyclopedias and the like, which couldn't be checked out. Jessie snapped the form onto her clipboard and stuck a pencil behind her ear. The phone on her desk rang.

"Library, Miss Holgrave here."

"Jessie, it's Ellen. He's trying to get in touch with you."

"Who?"

"Oh, for Pete's sake! Marsh, who else?"

"I don't want to talk to him."

"I know, but he called here last night practically in a panic. He's been trying to reach you since early Saturday morning. I told him you'd gone to your brother's place for the weekend, but that's all I said."

"He didn't need to know that much."

Ellen sighed. "Jessie, I don't know what's going on here, but I'm sure he cares about you."

"And you think I'm supposed to care about a man who could do what he did? Thanks a lot, Ellen, but I'm not that desperate, not yet."

"Okay, Jessie. I just thought you should know."

"I appreciate the call."

"Bye."

Jessie stood at her desk and stared out at the stunning spring day. The sun shone from a bright blue sky on healthy trees in full leaf. Cars drove in and out of the nearby neighborhood carrying people to work, off shopping, to appointments. It seemed strange that although a dark pall engulfed her own life, the rest of the world continued unchanged. Except for the world of a young man who'd been cruelly beaten, that is. His life would probably never be the same again. Jessie called the switchboard.

"Meg, this is Jessie. I'm starting my inventory, so please refuse any personal calls I might get. Just tell them I'm unavailable. Thanks."

On her way home, Jessie stopped at Radio Shack and bought an answering machine. She hooked it up to her telephone, then started a load of wash. The phone rang once and the machine clicked on. When the beep sounded, Marshall's voice filled the room.

"Jessie? What's going on? I've been trying to get you since Saturday morning. I know you were out of town, but I've got to talk to you. Things are heating up here and I won't have many more chances to call for quite a while. I'll try again about seven this evening. I love you."

Her arms crossed protectively over her waist, Jessie waited until he'd hung up before she approached the machine. Not that he could see her, but it felt that way. *Things are heating up*, he'd said. Grimly, Jessie thought she'd just bet they were. What did he expect when he'd been caught red-handed, flagrantly violating the Human

Rights Act? She pushed the button to rewind the tape.

At seven o'clock, Jessie was at the hamburger drive-in ordering a burger with everything, fries, and a milkshake. She ate her dinner in her parked car, then drove slowly home.

There were two messages on the machine, one from Marshall and one from Ellen. Marshall's consisted of a frustrated *where are you, are you all right, I love you* monologue. Ellen's was an invitation for dinner on Tuesday.

Neither Mike nor Ellen mentioned Marshall Abbott all during the meal. They both kept up a running recitation of life with Michelle and avoided asking Jessie about her day or her recent activities.

After dinner, Mike and Jessie worked in uncomfortable silence, cleaning up while Ellen nursed the baby. Mike cleared his throat. "Jessie, we've known each other nearly ten years, but I'll admit you've always been a mystery to me."

Jessie glanced at him out of the corner of her eye. "How so?"

Mike shrugged. "Well, here you are, one absolutely gorgeous woman, but you seldom go out with anyone."

Jessie gave Mike a sly grin. "Thanks for the

compliment, but beauty is only skin deep, you know. I don't have to tell you about my temper or my stubborn streak. Maybe no one wants the hassle."

Mike leaned against the sink and crossed his arms. "Oh, come on, Jessie. When we were in school there wasn't a guy on campus who wasn't dying to take you out, myself included."

"Really? Why didn't you ask me?" Jessie ask curiously.

"Because you had a reputation."

Jessie's face colored in embarrassment and anger, knowing young men would claim a score whether or not they'd even taken a girl out. Especially if she turned them down.

"No, not that kind," Mike snapped. "You were the ice princess; the queen of the black crystal cave; the cool, remote beauty with a tongue so sharp it could cut even the most secure jock to ribbons. And I was nowhere near secure enough to survive that."

"And then you met Ellen," Jessie grinned, remembering the moment. When she'd introduced them, Mike had stood speechless while Ellen's dimpled smile won his heart forever.

"Yeah," Mike sighed, returning the grin, "then I met Ellen. But you're trying to sidetrack me."

Jessie laughed. "It almost worked."

"Almost," Mike agreed. "So, back to you. I

know it's none of my business, but after all these years as friends, I'm curious."

Jessie carefully folded the dish towel as she considered how much to say. "Maybe most men don't outgrow their insecurities when it comes to a sharp-tongued woman."

"Some don't, but you're not that way, not really. I know you better than that now."

Jessie's chin came up defiantly. "Then maybe most men don't outgrow their inclination to take what they can and move on. And I won't settle for that."

Mike knew what he heard was as close to the truth as he'd get from Jessie. For a more detailed explanation he'd have to go to Ellen. He nodded in understanding. "Okay, good enough. In that case I don't blame you."

Relieved, Jessie turned to hang up the dish towel, but Mike wasn't finished. "But what about Marsh? He called me today pretty torn up. He can't get through to you at home or at school. I understand you've bought an answering machine, but I think it's really so you can avoid answering, isn't it, Jessie?"

Jessie refrained from looking at Mike and didn't reply.

"Jessie, he's in the field. Don't do this to him right now. I have no idea how you feel about him, but you're a pretty important person in Marsh's life, and at the moment that life is on the line. If you're going to dump on a cop, you don't do it when he's out there. It could get him killed."

Jessie's gaze darted to Mike's. She hadn't thought of that. Marshall Abbott had broken her heart—as well as a few laws—but she didn't want him dead. No, she surely didn't want that.

"Think about it," Mike instructed softly.

Jessie held Michelle, trying to urge a burp from the tiny frame while Ellen put clean sheets on the crib. Mike answered the telephone in the living room. A moment later he appeared at the nursery door.

"Jessie, it's for you."

She didn't have to ask who would be calling her here. She shook her head once.

"You have to, Jessie. Remember what I said."

She closed her eyes and swallowed at the lump in her throat. She couldn't do this, she just couldn't!

"Jessie," Mike's voice softly insisted.

She handed him his daughter with a sigh of resignation. Behind her, Mike and Ellen exchanged worried glances.

"Hello?"

"Jess? My God, Jess, it's good to hear your voice. Are you okay?"

"Of course." She struggled to keep her voice

neutral while thinking dismally, *He's very good at this. He really sounds as though he cares.*

"Jess, what's wrong? Talk to me."

The concern, the tenderness! He must have had the girls falling at his feet in school. Well, she knew better than to fall for his lines a second time. A costly lesson. Jessie had learned it well. She steeled her resolve and answered pleasantly, "I am talking to you, Marshall. I'm sorry I missed your earlier calls."

His voice took on an edge. "You are conversing with me, but you're not talking to me, Jess. Now, what is it? Have you found someone else?"

Jessie gave a cynical laugh. "Of course not. How could you think such a thing? There's no one quite like you, Marshall."

"Okay, Jess, something is bothering you big time and I want to know what it is."

Jessie's temper snapped. "All right," she agreed, her voice as smooth and cold as ice. "Let's just say I saw you on television the other night."

"The bust? You saw the bust?"

"Yes."

"Surely you don't think—"

"You don't want to know what I think, so don't push it," she retorted.

After a pause, Marshall replied, "I see. Well, that explains a lot." Jessie remained silent. A sigh drifted over the line, weary, heavy. "We need to talk, Jess, but I can see it'll have to wait until I get back. I love you."

Remembering Mike's words, Jessie suddenly felt panicked. "Marshall?"

"Yeah."

"Be careful."

"Yeah, sure." He hung up.

Mike pulled his shoulder away from the door frame as Jessie glanced around. "I didn't do very well, did I." It wasn't a question.

"No, not very, but I think I understand now, and Marsh probably does, too." Mike crossed his beefy arms over his chest and shook his head. "You're judging him by that videotape without even giving him the chance to defend himself."

Jessie studied her boots. What Mike's tone lacked in harshness, it made up for in disappointment. "Maybe you're right, maybe I should listen to what he has to say, but honestly, Mike, how do *you* justify what we saw?"

"I don't know, Jessie. I just hope Marsh gets the chance to try."

He turned and left the room and Jessie knew he referred to the danger of Marshall's assignment. Even though it was over between them, she prayed he would not be harmed.

Jessie sat in her porch swing thinking about what Mike had said while the wind chimes played with the edges of her mind. He'd called her an ice princess. He had no idea how far off target the ice image fell. As tenderhearted as the next woman, where Marshall Abbott had been concerned, her blood had run hot.

Queen of the black crystal cave, he'd said. She knew where that came from. It was a title from childhood, one Ellen had given her. They were twelve or thirteen and Ellen had been chosen to dance the Snow Queen in her ballet recital. Everyone, including Jessie, kept telling her how perfectly she fit the part, with her blond hair, blue eyes, and fair complexion. One day Ellen, sick of hearing it, exploded in frustration. "I don't *want* to be a wimpy, fluffy, snowflake of a person! I'd rather be like you, Jessie. You're tall and dark and dramatic. To anyone who doesn't know you, you're even kind of mysterious."

Jessie chuckled at the memory. How much mystery could there be in a twelve-year-old? She remembered denying it even then, but Ellen had insisted, "But you are! You keep your thoughts to yourself a lot, so people don't know what you're thinking, if you agree with them or not. You say I'm the perfect Snow Queen, but you know how I see you? I see you as the queen of a huge crystal cave, you know? Black crystals, hanging from the ceiling and sparkling on the walls. You sweep through it in a black velvet gown with a crystal crown on top of your smooth black hair and everybody stands back to watch you pass."

Ellen had heaved a heartfelt sigh and shaken her fluffy curls. "I'll never be thought of as dramatic or mysterious. I'm just cute and bubbly." Then she'd made a gagging motion and Jessie had laughed. For months after, they'd greeted each other as *Your Majesty*. Jessie hadn't thought about that in years.

Tall, *dark*, and *dramatic*. Ellen had left out *remote*, and *brittle*. But she hadn't been that way with Marshall and look what that had gotten her. *Dear God, keep him safe and heal my heart*, she prayed.

Chapter Eleven

A week and a half after the shattering news-cast, reports announced Marshall's suspension from duty pending an investigation. Jessie expected to hear from him then, and avoided answering the telephone until she knew the caller's identity, but he didn't call.

The school year drew to a close and still she didn't hear from him. She talked to Ellen two or three times a week, but refused to ask about him, and Ellen didn't offer any information. Except for the wind chime in the tree, Marshall Abbott might never have been a part of her life. Jessie went through her days the way she always had: alone. And lonely.

Her nights, however, were a different story.

171

The nightmares weren't as frequent now, dreams of Marshall's tender kisses more often than not replacing the chaotic scenes of brutality. But always a feeling of melancholy permeated these dreams, leaving Jessie unhappy and unsettled on waking, aware of a deep sense of loss.

Sunday afternoon she picked up Billy Stovall to take him to his new job. Even though Jim and Nonnie had been to visit with Billy's parents, she'd thought Billy would be less nervous if she brought him this first time.

They pulled into the driveway, Billy still talking a mile a minute, as he had ever since he'd climbed into the car. Jessie helped him unload his suitcase and a few possessions onto the porch, then Nonnie took over, sending Jessie up to see Jim while she directed Billy's move in.

"Jim?"

"I'm in here," came the voice from the stables.

Jessie found him examining the hoof of a bay gelding. "Brought your summer help," she greeted.

Jim dropped the horse's foot and straightened, engulfing Jessie in a fond hug. "Good, I'll get him busy first thing in the morning." He motioned to the animal tied to a post. "My newest pupil. They want me to make a cutting horse out of him."

Jessie ran a hand down the horse's neck and

over his shoulder. "He's certainly a handsome fellow."

Jim chuckled. Behind Jessie, a soft nickering caused her to turn. A horse had stuck his head over the gate of his stall and was stretching his neck out in a quest for attention.

"Scout," she breathed as her heart set up an erratic clatter. Her gaze swiveled to Jim. "Then he's back."

Jim nodded. "Yep, last night." He took a closer look at Jessie and frowned. "You all right, honey?"

"Ye . . . yes, I'm . . . I'm fine."

"Marsh mentioned something about needing to see you and straighten things out, but he didn't offer and I didn't ask."

Jessie didn't offer an explanation.

"He's probably still sleeping," Jim muttered as though to himself. "He was dead on his feet when he left here. Tried to get him to stay over, but he wouldn't do it."

Jessie reached out a tentative hand to scratch Scout's face.

"Fool kids," Jim muttered to himself and resumed checking over his new charge, leaving Jessie to her thoughts.

"I went by the house and she's not there. Has she taken off again?"

Mike shook his head. "I don't think so." He stepped back from the door and motioned Marsh inside. "Come on in and I'll ask Ellen."

"Ask me what? Oh, hello, Marsh."

"Do you know where Jessie is?"

"She drove out to Jim's, I think."

Marshall made a sound of frustration. "Now she'll know I'm back. I was hoping to get to her before she had a chance to start ducking me."

Ellen folded her lips in and bit down gently, keeping herself from speaking out of turn. Mike, however, wasn't as circumspect, asking, "What are you going to do?"

Marshall propped his hands on his hips and let his head fall back. "I don't know. Try to talk to her. I can't believe this is happening. I guess I don't know her after all."

Moved by the hurt in his voice, Ellen laid a hand on Marshall's arm. "Come and sit down a minute," she said softly.

Marshall didn't feel as comfortable with this little blond woman as he did with her husband, but Mike nodded to him encouragingly. "Go on. If you want answers, Ellen is your best chance to get them. No one else on earth is as close to Jessie as she is. I'll bring some coffee."

Ellen sat beside the large man and again laid a hand on his arm. "Tell me, what happened?"

"I'm not sure. I guess that newscast upset her."

"No, I mean what happened in San Isidro? Really."

"Mike didn't tell you?"

Mike entered the room and handed Marshall a mug of coffee. "I haven't had the chance. I just got home fifteen minutes ago, and the official report was just passed on to us this afternoon."

"It was staged," Marshall began. He explained the events to Ellen. The he said, "I can't believe Jess didn't trust me more than that. She sure had no trouble jumping to the wrong conclusion."

Ellen sighed and patted his arm. "Marsh, you need to remember that before you left, she'd only known you a month. Four weeks, Marsh, that's all. Aren't you asking a lot based on such a short acquaintance?"

"You either trust someone or you don't! Obviously, she didn't!"

Ellen glanced at her husband, then back at Marshall. Quickly she weighed her loyalty to Jessie against her friend's ultimate happiness. "That's not quite true, is it, Marsh?" she asked softly. "Do you know her area of sensitivity?"

Marshall looked at Ellen, then dropped his gaze. "You mean her distrust of Caucasian men?"

Ellen nodded. "And lawmen. Her brothers were hassled quite a bit as teens. Sometimes with cause, most of the time not. In fact, it still happens from time to time."

"Yeah, but . . ."

"It's pretty deep-seated," Ellen interrupted softly. "She loves you, but what she saw on television scared her to death. She doesn't trust her instincts. It really isn't you she doesn't trust, it's herself. She lacks the confidence to trust her own judgment, Marsh."

"Why, for Pete's sake?"

"I don't know." Ellen shrugged. "Why are some people chatterboxes and some silent as stone? Why do some people have dimples and some freckles?" Ellen abruptly changed directions. "How do you feel about her, deep down, I mean?"

Marshall looked down at his large hands, dangling loosely between his knees. "You want to know if I really care for her," he replied flatly. Ellen nodded and he sighed. "I care how she's getting along, I care whether she's been hurt by this."

Ellen's expression reflected her annoyance, and Marshall shot her a sideways grin.

"But you asked about deep down, didn't you?" Edgy, he rose to his feet and crossed to the window. With his fingers shoved into his back pockets, he stared out over the deck and the shady backyard. "Deep down, I'd just as soon have died and my body laid unclaimed under that south Texas sun than lose Jess. I love her, Ellen. I thought I'd been in love a couple of times before, but now I know different. Now I *know* what it is to love someone, and Jess is that someone. I can't lose her, I can't."

Ellen wiped a tear from her eye and gave an embarrassed chuckle. "Well, you've convinced me. Now let's see what you can do about Jessie."

Jessie eased her car onto her lane, checking to make sure no Jeep sat in front of her house. None did and she sighed in relief. She'd spent the night with Jim and Nonnie, then come home after a late breakfast. She refused to feel guilty about her cowardice.

Nan ambled around the house and stood waiting patiently for her to let him in and feed him. Jessie took care of that chore, then opened the back door to let Sheba out, freezing in place when a masculine voice drawled, "Good morning."

Marshall unfolded from a lounge chair on the patio, running his fingers through his tousled hair. His clothing was wrinkled and he needed a shave. His hazel eyes were weary and underscored by dark circles. But even as her heart cramped in pain at having to face him, Jessie thought he looked wonderful.

"Where's your car?"

"Behind your garage."

"Why?"

The look he gave her plainly said, *Don't play the fool!* Marshall took a step toward her and Jessie quickly retreated, closing the screen door firmly. "Jess, we have to talk."

"There's nothing to say."

"Look, I spent the night sleeping on your patio instead of my nice comfortable bed just so I could have the chance to explain. I think you owe me that much at least."

"I don't know that I owe you anything, Mr. Abbott. You got what you were after, didn't you?"

His tone slightly menacing, Marshall gritted, "No, Jess, I haven't, not yet."

"Then that's just too bad!"

She started to close the door, but Marshall leaped up the two steps, pulled the screen open, and pushed his way into the house.

Jessie yelped and stumbled back, but he grabbed her arms to keep her from falling. The terror in her eyes and the trembling of her body beneath his hands made Marshall angry.

"Blast it, Jess, I'm not going to hurt you! You should know that by now!" His voice softened as he pleaded, "I just want to talk. Please?"

Jessie swallowed at the panic that clogged her throat and chest and nodded.

"That's better. Now let's go sit down."

He kept hold of one arm and led her into the living room, where he dropped to the sofa, pulling her down with him. She tugged at her arm but didn't move away when he let her go.

"Now," he began, his voice low, "tell me exactly what it is you're so upset about."

With a gasp of disbelief, Jessie sprang from the couch, but Marshall caught her arm and tugged her back down.

"Jess! Of course I know in general terms, but I want to hear it from you. I want to address your concerns one at a time."

Struggling to control her outrage, Jessie took several deep breaths until she felt capable of speaking rationally. Her heart was breaking even as fury accelerated her pulse to a dizzying level. She'd be lucky to verbalize her own name, let alone her thoughts and feelings about what he'd done in San Isidro. Marshall waited patiently.

"Okay," she said at last, "I'll try. I saw the video on television. The one taken by a tourist. I saw you and another man, a Ranger I think, kick a fallen man. I saw you beat him."

Marshall's head dropped back to rest on the sofa as he closed his eyes. "And you believed it," he whispered.

"I didn't want to, but I saw it, Marsh, I saw *you*."

Marshall sighed. "Then what?"

"Then I ran to the bathroom and heaved my insides out," Jessie muttered.

Marshall opened his eyes and saw her arms crossed tightly over her waist. She had one corner of her bottom lip caught in her teeth and tears filled her eyes. He lifted a hand and brushed his knuckles against her cheek.

"Jess, it's not what you think."

She recoiled from his touch. "Oh, Marsh, I can understand how things might get out of hand, those are terrible people you were after, but I heard what you said, too. I heard what you called him!"

"And?"

"And I wondered how long it would be before you thought of me that way, called me names, looked at me with loathing."

"Jess, never," he protested. "How could you even think it?"

She shrugged and looked away. He sat forward and took one of her hands in his. Jessie tried to pull free, but he held it in a firm grip.

"No, Jess, I haven't gotten what I want," he said, going back to her earlier comment. "I want you. Forever. But that's not going to happen until we clear up this misunderstanding."

"Misunderstanding! Is that what you call it?"

"Yes. And I think it's only fair to tell you how much your lack of faith hurts. When I called you, it never occurred to me that you'd believe all that propaganda. It nearly killed me that you did."

Jessie's startled gaze met his and her breath caught. "I . . . I didn't want you hurt. I mean, shot or anything."

A wry smile lifted one corner of Marshall's mouth. "Thanks," he said with sarcasm.

"I didn't."

"I know. Anyway, Ellen pointed out that you'd only known me a few weeks and that's not much time to overcome years of mistrust, so I'm trying to be understanding. But it still hurts, Jess."

"I'm sorry, but I can't work up much guilt at hating the sight of you committing such violence on an unarmed man. Even if he were white, what makes you think I could welcome you into my life with that kind of blood on your hands? I thought you were gentle and kind. How could I be so wrong?"

Jessie covered her face with her hands and leaned her elbows on her knees. She made no sound, but he knew she was weeping. He lifted his hand and stroked her head tenderly.

"Jess? It was staged—make-believe. Planned, all of it. To the last detail."

She sniffed. "What are you talking about?"

"Didn't you stop to wonder what a 'tourist' was doing hanging around a warehouse that time of night?"

"Well, no."

"Did you actually see my fist connect with the man's face?"

"No. But I saw the two of you kicking him."

"The blows were pulled, we barely touched him. Just enough to leave bruises."

"How kind of you," she snorted.

"If he didn't have any marks on him, the people he reported to would have killed him. Jess, the man on the ground was a Ranger. He infiltrated the coyote's ring. We rounded up several of the operatives that night, but still needed the big man. We had to make it look good. That's the reason for the videotape."

Jessie studied his eyes a moment, trying to find the truth there. In her own, Marshall saw nothing but doubt.

"What about your suspension?"

"Bogus. I didn't come back to town, did I?"

"I don't know, you could have."

"True, but I didn't. With Ray's help, I tracked that everlovin' scum down and we busted him. We caught him, Jess," he exclaimed and there was no mistaking the triumph in his eyes. "And as soon as he was behind bars, I hightailed it back to you."

He slipped his hand under Jessie's heavy fall of hair and his fingers caressed the nape of her neck. "I'm tired, I'm sore, and I'm frustrated. But none of that is as bad as being so heartsick. I love you, Jess. I want to hold you."

He felt her tense under his hand. "I didn't do those things," he whispered. "You could never love a man like that and you do love me. You told me so. That should be all the proof you need."

A shudder passed through Jessie's body and suddenly she was racked with sobs.

"Hey, hey." He pulled her into his arms. "Don't cry, sweetheart. Please, don't cry."

"Oh M—Marsh, I'm . . . I'm sorry. It was all so hor—horrible," she cried. "It fel—felt like you'd kicked *m*—*me*, and I di—didn't know wh . . . what to think."

"Shhh, it's okay now."

"No it's not! I've hurt you and nearly destroyed myself!"

"What do you mean?" he snapped.

"No, not that." Jessie wiped her eyes and her voice grew stronger. "I just felt that my life was over, that I'd died inside. When the shock wore off, I . . . I realized I loved you anyway, even though I couldn't accept you back." She drew a shaky breath and sniffled. "I couldn't reconcile that within myself. I've been worried sick about you and so torn up inside because of it."

"Poor mixed-up Jess." He kissed her temple. "You need to trust yourself more, as well as me."

"Marsh . . ."

She looked up as she spoke, giving him the opening he'd waited for. His lips cut off her words. Several minutes later, when they both labored for breath, he raised his head again. "How about . . ."

A knock at the door cut Marshall off. Jessie rose to answer it, Nan trotting close to her side.

"Morning, Jessie. There's someone I'd like you to meet."

Mike Sanders stood on her front porch with a young man who looked vaguely familiar. "This is Texas Ranger Ray Ortiz. Ray, Jessie Holgrave, the woman who's driving Marsh crazy these days."

"Mike!" Jessie scolded as a heavy blush sizzled its way up her neck.

Ray pretended not to notice and held out his hand, a warm grin lighting his face. "Pleased to meet you, Miss Holgrave. It's easy to see why Marsh acts a little distracted from time to time."

Jessie shook the man's hand with a mumbled "thank you," and was about to invite them in when Marshall's warm hands cupped her shoulders. She hadn't heard him come up behind her.

"I thought I heard my name being defamed," he greeted. "What's this, an invasion?"

"Naw." Mike looked a little self-conscious. "Just a small rescue operation. Sorry, I didn't see your Jeep."

The men filed in and Marshall explained, "I hid it from Jessie."

Mike nodded. When Jessie went to the kitchen for coffee, he whispered, "It's okay now? You've got it all straightened out?"

Marsh gave a short dry chuckle. "I think so, but thanks for bringing the cavalry."

Ray grinned again. "Hey, no problem, *amigo*. If she doesn't believe you, maybe *I* can ask her out?"

Marshall threw a small pillow at Ray's head and growled, "You're too short. And if I catch you anywhere near her, you'll be a whole lot shorter, if you know what I mean."

"Man," Ray grumbled, "talk about police brutality."

"Jess, you okay with this now?"

They were sitting on the porch swing, listening to the evening breeze as it played in the wind chimes. Jess stirred as she snuggled in the crook of his arm and sighed. She picked up the hand that rested on his thigh and wove her fingers through his, squeezing tightly.

"Jess?"

"I still feel awful," she murmured. "I hurt inside."

The arm around her shoulders tightened and Marsh kissed her temple, then caressed it lightly with his lips. "Tell me about it?"

"You might have been killed and all I could think about was how badly you'd deceived me."

"It's over, let it go."

"How can you be so blasé? I let you down, I didn't believe in you."

"Do you love me, Jess?"

"You know I do."

"Then put it behind us. A few months from now you won't have any doubts at all, but I'm not about to throw away the best thing that's ever come my way just because you didn't know me well enough yet to withstand some pretty incriminating evidence."

Marshall's arm held her firmly to his side as he bent to nuzzle her ear. "Can you really forgive me, just like that?"

"Just like that," came the husky whisper.

His warm breath sent shivers down her spine and Jessie lifted her face for a kiss. Marshall gladly obliged, then whispered against her hair, "Summer's a great time for weddings, don't you think?"